NOTHING IN THE SKY BUT AIR

His mind was whirling through the universe, when hers was stuck firmly on planet earth.

ELEANOR GARVEY

For my friends, the best I could ask for.

*If love could have saved you
you would have lived forever*

-unknown

One

The problem with falling in love is that sometimes one person will fall harder than the other. Eden fell, too hard. And it was over before she could stop it. You see the issue here is that she didn't know what she was doing until it was too late. It was out of her control. Like when you light a fire and it just continues to grow and grow and you don't know how to stop it. She had her heart broken into a million different pieces, and there was no way to put it back together again. She had created a puzzle that was impossible to solve.
Eden lay on her friend's sofa, it was brown and had these uncomfortable pillows on that looked like the type you'd find in your grandmother's house. She woke up and lay there, her feet dangling over the edge and her head propped up on the arm rest. There was a strong smell of coffee throughout the apartment that was just begging for her to follow into the kitchen. But she couldn't. She couldn't move from the warmth of the blanket which was meagerly covering her limp body. There was faint, slightly out of tune singing coming from one room which she could

just about hear, not very good singing of course, but somewhat entertaining. Eventually she managed to heave herself off the sofa and move herself into the kitchen where Juliet sat eating a bowl of cereal and drinking, as Eden had guessed, coffee. The two of them had been friends since they were kids. Always messing around, they spent nearly every day of those eighteen years they had together, until graduation came around, before attempting to go their separate ways. It didn't last. Juliet was stunningly gorgeous, she had big curly hair and dark toned skin which glowed whenever the sun came out. It glowed any day of the week to be honest, but Eden thought it was extra beautiful in the sun.

'Morning,' Juliet said, smiling and picking up her abnormally large mug of steaming coffee.

'Hi,' Eden mumbled quietly. Her face looked cold and she had dark bags under her eyes, which Juliet had noticed they had been there continuously for the past three weeks. She knew everything was okay, yet she also knew nothing was okay. If there was anything Juliet had learned, it was that being okay was just enough, because we don't wish for fantastic or marvellous knowing that it will come easily. Okay was just enough to keep us going. Eden was unusually reserved and sombre. She never cared about her appearance now, she barely left the apartment, and she rarely ate. It was clear in her stance. Her skin clung to her bones like it was the only way of surviving and you could count each rib on your fingers.

'You okay?' Juliet asked, almost knowing what the answer was going to be. The same every time. A simple 'yes' and then she would walk out of the kitchen, back onto the sofa, or into the bathroom and she wouldn't see her for the rest of the day until she got back from her classes.

'I'm fine.' Eden poured herself a glass of water from the tap and pulled up a chair opposite her friend. Juliet was shocked, but she didn't show it. By now there was no point showing emotions, it would only make Eden even more anxious and upset.

'That's the most recent New York Times, if you're interested.' Juliet pointed to the newspaper sitting halfway across the table. Making conversation was hard nowadays. She couldn't just talk about any random thing, it could set Eden off.

'So I've got classes all morning, but I'm free for lunch, if you want to meet somewhere. We could grab a bagel or something?' Juliet asked. Her spoon clashed against the bowl and made Eden wince.

'Sure.' Eden produced a weak smile which lasted for a tenth of a second, before resuming her current state of solemnness.

'Okay, well I'll meet you outside Seth's Sandwiches around one?' Juliet suggested before standing up from her chair and placing her empty bowl and mug in the sink that was stacked full of dirty dishes. Eden nodded. She tucked her sandy blonde hair behind both ears. It was thin and needed washing. Her face looked hollow and sunken in, like it was illegal that there was any life in it for a matter of fact. Around her, Juliet gathered up the things she needed to take to class.

'Alright,' Juliet kissed Eden on the top of her head, 'I'm going to head out now. Do something useful,' she pointed at Eden as she walked backwards towards the door. Then pulling her keys out she proceeded to unlock the door and swung it open. 'Bye,' she said.
'Why do you care about me so much?' Eden suddenly asked. Juliet stopped in her tracks and looked down at her feet. Of course she knew what she wanted to say. She didn't want Eden going off the tracks and taking her own life. She knew it would happen if she was all alone. But she couldn't say that. Not in front of her.
Juliet turned around and sighed.
'Because I love you. I've really got to go, but I'll see you at lunch.' She waved goodbye and closed the door behind her. Eden could picture her smile even after she left, because it made her so incredibly wanted.
Eden sat there staring at the table, tracing her finger over the wooden marks that were stained on it. She stood up slowly and shuffled into the bathroom, taking in a deep breath of disgustingly warm air. The windows were steamed and it was awkwardly warm in there. She wiped away a small part of the mirror so she could see herself properly. Her face was pale and unhealthy looking, there were blue veins marked in her skin and her eyes were blank. She hated herself. Everything about her. A tear rolled down from her eye. Eden noticed it and wiped it away imminently. And then it hit her. Why had she wiped it away? There was no one in the apartment who could see her. Who cared what she looked like at that moment in time? She let the tears roll down her cheek, one after the

other. It was like a rainstorm on her face, they kept on coming. The thunder, the loud cries she made as she looked up into the mirror and saw what was reflecting back at her. Why was she even here? Eden thrust open the cabinet door and began emptying it out. She wasn't sure what she was trying to find... something to take away the pain that she felt. There was a yellow tube filled with tablets, the label had been ripped off, maybe they were old, or unused, or both?
Eden desperately opened the tube and poured them out into her hand. She ran into the kitchen and picked up the glass of water she had left on the table, and then dumped the pills in her mouth like they were a handful of candy. She downed the water soon after before leaning down on the table on her elbow and closing her eyes. She was breathing heavily. Too heavily. She stumbled back into the bathroom and closed the door. That was it. If that didn't work she didn't know what would. Surely that should ease the pain. Stop everything from hurting. Wasn't that what drugs were supposed to do? Stop the pain?
When she was five years old Eden asked her mum what happened when you died. Did you go somewhere else? Or did your eyes just blackout and you went blind? Her mum told her that you went somewhere special that no one knew of. It was just there.
Her breath was warm and heavy. You could see the sweat rolling down from her face and onto her clothes. She lay there across the bathroom floor, her head somewhat propped up against the side of the bath. Everything she had pulled out of the cabinet was spread across the floor

in front of her, bottles of shampoo, a first aid kit, and the now empty bottle of pills she had just poisoned her body with. Her eyes suddenly went blurry and her head was throbbing, like the kind when you had a migraine and you actually couldn't cope with the pain.
'Juliet,' she thought she cried out, but no words came out of her mouth. Juliet wasn't in the apartment to start with. Her cries were silent. They always had been. Eden lay there on the hard floor unable to move, or get up. Her body had frozen with pain. She had gone bright red in the face and you could feel the heat radiating off of her cheeks if you stood near her. There was mystery behind her, because she didn't know what she was doing, and neither did anyone else. Her mind was off somewhere in an alternate universe that no one could understand.
All was quiet, and then even quieter.

Love makes you do stupid things. But cosmic love makes you so obsessed and in love with someone that it seems nothing else matters. It's a love with so much emotion that it becomes incredibly unique and special. Can cosmic love be broken? Everything ends eventually doesn't it? Nothing lasts forever. Even if you think it does. One day the universe will just evaporate into thin air as the sun sets for the very last time. It will fall into a void of nothingness, yet it will rise into an abyss of everything. As you fall asleep for the last time, you will never wake up. It's a bit like love. One day it will all come to an end, if it's tomorrow, or on your deathbed. Nothing lasts forever.

Cosmic love comes with two things. Fate and luck. Fate brings you together. Up in the sky there is a magnet that guides you together, and when it meets, it sticks. They attract, they don't retract. Yet it's also luck that they remain together. Some magnets are stronger than others. Some love is stronger than other love. And sometimes, cosmic love just doesn't exist. Magnets stick together, and then fall apart when they've lost all of their pull. Love draws two people together, yet sometimes time outruns them and they fall apart. Time always wins. Why can't some people understand that? The magnets in the sky control our destiny, not ourselves. They play us, and move us in all different ways until we become so tired of their games that we want to take a break. And we fall.

Seth's Sandwiches was a small independent cafe in the East Village of New York. The menu was small, but that's what made it so special. Juliet had arrived five minutes before one. Eden would be here soon. It was a cooler, wetter, more dismal day in New York City. January was never the nicest month of the year. The sky was coloured with grey clouds and cried tears of pure water. She put down her umbrella and opened the door to go inside.
It was a rustic cafe, with old wooden chairs and tables, and yellow lights that hung low from the ceiling. The walls were a faded teal colour with miscellaneous paintings and photos hung up on the walls randomly. Juliet always sat by the far right window that overlooked Tompkins Square Park. Obviously there was hardly anyone in the park, it

was a wet rainy day. She couldn't get hold of Eden. Her phone went straight to voicemail.

'Hi what can I get for you today?' A young man walked up to her and stood overlooking the table. All Juliet could focus on was the red bandana he had tied around his neck, it was the brightest thing she's seen all day.

'Oh, can you hold on for five more minutes, I'm waiting for a friend.' She asked. He nodded and walked away back to the counter. It had gone one. Eden should be here. Usually, she was never late. But then, they were living in unusual times. Juliet looked around the cafe, checking if maybe she hadn't seen her yet, but she wasn't there. The cafe music played in the background, it was the old stuff that your parents like to listen to. She leant against her chair and waited.

Eden never came. Juliet ate her lunch in silence, alone. It wasn't the first time, and definitely wouldn't be the last. Of course Eden wouldn't come though. Physically, she couldn't. Mentally, she probably wouldn't come either. The small cafe emptied out of all the people stopping by for lunch. There was a small pile of books she had pulled out of her bag, a notebook where she had kept her notes for the mornings classes, and her laptop which was covered in an array of colourful stickers she had collected over the years. Since she was ten she had wanted to study English Literature in New York. There wasn't a moment you didn't see her carrying around at least one book. Always stuck in a book was she, looking for adventure, excitement, something different. Well, at least she had got something different out of moving to New

York. A very hurt, depressed, lonely best friend who rarely spoke to her and who skipped out on lunch dates to do the same thing she always did. Sit on the sofa and watch TV. Except, she wasn't doing what she always did.

Eden lay across the bathroom floor. She was surrounded by a mess of empty, full, half empty, bottles and tubs of bathroom products. Her hair was spread under her small, blank face and her eyes were shut tight. There was no life in her. If you saw her you would think she was truly and utterly gone. Her chest didn't beat up and down, it was still. The bathroom window was steamed up, the mirror had patchy finger prints on, and there was a girl, lying there, lifeless, hollow, and alone. Love makes you do such fucking crazy things sometimes because you can't think straight. She lay there, and entered a world of her own for a little while. Her breath was almost unhearable, her heart was barely beating, and her lungs were hardly breathing.

Two

Juliet finished her food, packed up, and left. Why was she not surprised that Eden had bailed on her again? She could just picture Eden lying on the sofa, watching TV and doing absolutely nothing, knowing that she had flaked out on leaving the apartment for the first time in weeks. Her hair was speckled with the rain drops that fell from the sky, and her coat covered her dry clothes, it was cold and wet, and made everything seem grey. She wanted the dismal days to be over, because maybe Eden would be less dismal. Juliet longed for the day when Eden smiled again.

She enjoyed the walk back to her apartment. The air was still cool and damp, she let it refresh her face as she continued to make her way down the street. The roads were somewhat busy, loud noise circulated the city, but then, this was the city that never sleeps. There wasn't a time in the day when there weren't loud noises. Eventually she turned the corner to her apartment complex and walked up the metal stairs. She and Eden were on the fifth floor, the walk wasn't too far up. If anything, it was relaxing

to feel like she had done some form of exercise despite walking the streets of New York.
She pulled out the key from her bag and opened the door. Eden wasn't on her usual sofa, or at the kitchen table.
'Eden!' Juliet called out as she shut the door behind her, took her coat off and placed her bag on the coffee table by the sofa. There was no answer. Had she gone out? There was no reason for her to go out. She rarely left the apartment as it was. Juliet called out again, and again there was no answer. Something caught her eye. An empty glass was rolling about on the floor underneath the kitchen table, and next to it, a tablet. Just one. But she had never taken a tablet that looked like that before. The bottle had been placed at the back of the bathroom cabinet, unopened. There was a crack in the glass where it had been dropped onto the floor, as Juliet picked it up it broke in her hands, splintering glass all over the floor.
It suddenly hit her that Eden could have put it there. By accident. The bathroom door was closed, but not locked. Juliet rushed to the door and threw it open. Before she opened it she knew what she was going to find. A girl, lying across the bathroom floor. Maybe dead? Maybe not. The bathroom cabinet's contents were scattered across the floor, and an empty bottle of pills right by Eden's hand. Juliet stood there in shock, she was scared, afraid, and then she was in absolute tears. Had her best friend just killed herself? She had blue lips that looked like they had just been covered in blue freshaid, and her eyes were shut tight, but Juliet didn't even want to look at them, she was scared at what would be behind.

The ambulance arrived soon after to take Eden away to the hospital. Juliet climbed into the back with her, she had wrapped her coat around herself and sat in the back shivering. Goosebumps formed on her skin, and her legs bounced up and down as she sat watching them save Eden. But what if they didn't? She had done everything she could do. She had followed the instructions given by the ambulance before it had arrived, nothing worked. Juliet looked at Eden's blank face, her eyes were shut tightly and all the life had been sucked out of her. You could see the blue veins in her head and neck and on her eyelids too. She looked cold, she felt cold. Juliet took Eden's hand as it fell off of the small bed she was lying on. It was icy, and sent a chill through Juliet's back. The nails in her fingers had gone blue. The colour you see when you look out across the sea at around 3pm. She wiped away a tear that had emerged from her eye. But it wasn't enough.
'Ma'am if you could just move to one side please,' one of the doctors asked. Juliet let go of Eden's hand and slid across to one side where she brought her knees up to her chest and dug her face onto her knees. She wanted to cry, she needed to cry, but now just wasn't the right time. Was there ever a right time?
The rest of the day flashed before Juliet's eyes. There were moments when she wasn't sure what was going on, moments when she knew what was happening but didn't want to know, and moments that she didn't even process properly. It was like the whole world was in time lapse but her, and they didn't even bother to wait for her. The

waiting room at the hospital was bright and smelt of freshly sanitized surfaces. Bleach mainly. There were white faux leather chairs placed in two U shapes and potted green plants in the corners of the room. The window was open, but the dismal daylight had elapsed into a dismal dark night. The only light came from the bright, but fake, lights which were hanging from the high ceilings of the hospital.

There was no knowing how long she sat there in the waiting room. She had run all her change down that she had found in her coat pocket on the vending machine opposite her. There were now empty packets of chocolate bars and a bottle of coke sitting in her lap. Juliet watched people come and go. She even recognised one person from one of her classes that she had that very morning.

'Jason, what are you doing here?' she asked as he walked past her heading for the exit. He stopped in his tracks and turned to face her.

'Oh um... my Grandma is here, she's sick. Really sick.' He sat down on the chair next to Juliet and brought his legs up to cross them.

'I'm sorry to hear that,' Juliet replied, rubbing his shoulder. They were friends, they had met at the beginning of the school year in September. Although they didn't speak often, they had a strange connection that made them get along well.

'No it's fine. She's been here for a while, it's only a matter of time,' he said and shrugged his shoulders.

'It always is,' Juliet muttered. Time really was all some people had, and it played people like a fool. One moment

everything is fine, and then time catches up and kills everything. Sometimes it kills people.
'Anyway, why are you here?' He asked, taking the bottle of coke from her lap and having a sip.
'Um, Eden, my friend from back home...' she started before he interrupted her.
'The one who is like major depressed because she broke up with that rock god boyfriend?' He asked.
'That's the one. She had an accident.' Juliet replied. She didn't want to get into any detail. The less people knew about it the better.
'What kind of accident?'
This question was almost fated. She wouldn't answer it. Not how he wanted to hear it at least.
'I'd rather keep the details under wraps, if that's okay?'
She too crossed her legs on the chair and brought the blanket up to her shoulders that she had wrapped around her body.
'Sure, that's totally cool,' he said agreeingly. The one thing about Jason that Juliet loved was how caring he was for his friends and how you could trust him with absolutely anything.
'Thanks Jas,' she smiled and reached out to hug him over the chair.
'But if there's anything you need,' he quickly whispered into her ear.
'I'll call you.' She hugged tighter. He was warm, wrapped up in his thick winter coat. She pulled away and he stayed for a little longer. They talked about class, about how much they hated most of the people in their class, about

what they'd do if they won the lottery. Juliet had never noticed how green his eyes were. They were bright and soft all at once. They carried a caring glow that almost hypnotised you into looking into them. And when he smiled his cheeks went up and they seemed even more beautiful. He had hair like a fresh winter morning. Crisp and neatly placed like the snow fallen on the ground. He cared about his appearance which was one of the most important qualities someone could have, Juliet thought. She had never looked at him this way before. There's no time like the present.

'Will you be in class tomorrow?' He asked as they neared the end of their conversation.

'Probably not,' Juliet shrugged. She tucked her sweeping hair behind both ears to move it out of the way. Her ears were covered in piercings all the way to the top. Some piercings like that didn't suit people, but on Juliet, they defined who she was.

'Well, like I said, I'm always here. I'll see you soon.' He stood up and wiped down anything that had somehow fallen onto his lap.

'Bye,' she said as she looked up into his eyes again.

'Bye.' He walked away out of the door and onto the street opposite. She watched him until he was no more than a speck in the distance. He blended in quite well to the dark night that had fallen over the city.

And so she was back to being alone, again. Her mind wandered in and out of Jason, Eden, home. It was a continuous loop. He managed to work his magic ways back into her mind when she should be thinking about

Eden. Eden. She forgot. She had been so encased in talking to Jason that she had forgotten to check if Eden was okay.

Juliet followed the nurse that led her through the maze that was the hospital to Eden's room. There was a thin tube up Eden's nose and she lay there in a white and blue hospital gown. It wasn't the sight she wanted to see. Eden's eyes were still closed, but the nurse told Juliet that she was conscious, she was probably just asleep.

Juliet walked in and sat on the chair next to Eden's As she explored the room from her seat she clearly managed to work out why people bring flowers to hospitals. They were so devoid of beauty that they needed something to make them look somewhat pretty. And the most beautiful thing a person can do is create natural beauty in a place where beauty was forbidden. No wonder people slept when they were in hospital. They couldn't bear to look around a room of plain nothing. There were no decorations on the wall. They were painted an off brand white, nothing special. There never was anything special about a hospital bed. They simply closed their eyes to pass the time of lying in complete silence whilst people hurried back and forth with drugs that were supposed to heal a person inside. Did they ever heal someone properly though? There would always be a part of that person that knew they had to spend a night in a house of barren alienation.

Eden's eyes flickered like the flickering of an old TV turning on. They wandered around, looking up and down, left and right. She slowly turned her head to face Juliet who had dozed off in her chair. Eden reached out for a

part of Juliet to hold. Her leg was stretched out underneath Eden's bed. Eden's hand stretched out to brush against Juliet's knee. She shuddered and then opened her eyes to look directly into Eden's.
Eden tried to produce a smile, but she was still too weak. Instead she just took Juliet's warm hand as Juliet moved in closer towards her.
'Hey...' Juliet whispered quietly. She knelt down beside Eden.
'Hi,' Eden mouthed. She couldn't quite produce any words yet, but Juliet could make out what she was trying to say.
'You really scared me you know. What were you trying to do?' Juliet asked. She brought her hand up to Eden's cold cheek and caressed it.
Eden attempted a shrug of the shoulders. Already her face had more life in it than it had ever had these past few weeks.
'I called your mum too, she said she'd be down as soon as possible,' Juliet added. Eden nodded and took a deep breath through the tube that was stuffed up her nose. She managed to move her other hand to clasp around her right hand which held tightly onto Juliet's.
It was a quiet night. It went slowly, people came in and out of the room. Juliet was told to go home, and despite her wishes and intentions, she did. She called a taxi to collect her from the hospital and she was driven back to the apartment. She could've walked, it would've been nice to get the fresh air after being locked up in the hospital for so long.

What made a person hate their life so much that they wanted to end it? Was it the constant suppressive nature of not living up to people's standards? On this occasion, Juliet knew why. If anything, there had always been a small part in her mind that knew something like this would happen. It was only a matter of time, she repeated. For the past three weeks Eden had been living in a shell of depression, it was all she knew. All of the wicked thoughts that had been said about her were trapped in this bubble around her, and they hacked at her brain so much that it finally broke her into a million pieces. And the problem? This puzzle could never be fixed. They had shattered into too many pieces. They had shattered too far apart to ever be brought back together. No one could ever be brought back together fully. Because glue one day breaks and falls apart, just like everything else.

Three

After the incident, things changed. Juliet had noticed that Eden was more active, she got up earlier, she even went on a run every morning around the park. She ate three meals a day, which was three more than what she was originally eating. The black circles under her eyes had evaporated and had been replaced with brightness. Her face was perkier and rosier, like spring had finally decided to come, despite it still being bleak winter. They had cleared space in the small living room and bought a proper bed for Eden to sleep on, instead of curling up every night on the uncomfortable sofa she had been sleeping on. Life had flattened out slightly, everything seemed to go a little smoother than before. There was a record shop down the street that Eden managed to get a job at. She stacked and reordered the shelves filled with vintage records that people had donated. It smelt of old dust, but that's what she so dearly loved about it.
'So I was thinking, I might apply for NYU, you know, see if I can get a degree,' Eden said as the two were sitting

down one evening having just brought in a bag full of chinese food.

'Why the sudden change of heart? You never wanted to go to university before,' Juliet asked as she processed the information she had just been told. Even in high school she had never even considered getting a degree. Then, there was a reason for that.

'I want to do something, I get bored. Sure I've got a job, but I want the satisfaction of doing something more,' Eden explained. She tucked her hair behind her ears and placed her elbows on the table in front of her.

'What would you even study?' Juliet laughed as she ate another mouthful of food.

'Well, music, performance. Maybe something to do with that,' she shrugged and smiled. Juliet tried to keep in her laugh, but she couldn't. She burst out of laughing. Eden glared at her. 'Wow, I thought you'd be a bit more supportive.' Eden stood up and walked out of the room onto her bed.

'No no I am,' Juliet followed her and sat down next to her on the bed. 'I just never thought I'd see the day when you'd pick up another textbook. I'm proud of you.' Juliet patted Eden's back, before leaning in for a hug.

'I've been here doing nothing for weeks, and I hate it. Maybe it's time I just... loosen up a bit. Besides, I never hated school,' she smirked.

'I know you never hated it, you were one of the smartest there,' Juliet pointed out. Eden gave Juliet a kind of *what are you fucking on about* look.

The following day was a Thursday. Eden was in the record shop, alone. The owner was out on his lunch break. A thin layer of snow had fallen that night, but the heavy feet of New York had practically pushed it to the sides of the road and into the gutters. So, again, it looked like another dismal rainy January afternoon. She sat in the corner of the box shaped shop sorting through a pile of old David Bowie records that had been dropped off the previous week. Most records in the shop were ordered alphabetically by artist. Bowie was right at the beginning, she picked up the pile and shuffled across the room to where she would file them, brushing off the dust from the shelf and wheezing when it went up her nose. There were a couple of new Justin Bieber records and some Bee Gees albums which had collected dust over the years. Eden slotted the Bowie records into place, dusted her hands off and went to sit by the counter where she put the old glitchy radio on. Her phone vibrated in her pocket.
How do you feel about having someone over for dinner tonight? -J
Eden stared at the message. Surely it wouldn't be that bad. Besides, Juliet's friends were kept to a minimum, and they certainly wouldn't be crazy, that wasn't Juliet's type.
Go for it. Who are we taking? Eden replied. She left her phone on the counter as she pulled out a box under that was filled with a random selection of artists.
Jason, he's chill. -J
Okay :) Eden texted back. As long as she didn't have to cook anything, she'd be fine. Cooking wasn't exactly her strongest.

The door opened and the small bell rang to let Eden know someone had just arrived. It was only Mr Shore, the owner. He was old, too old to still be running a business in fact. His grey hair had almost disappeared from his head. He carried a cardboard box that was almost tearing apart because of how wet it was. Mr Shore always wore these old vintage sweater vests, he had them in every colour you could imagine, and they always smelled of home. Freshly burnt fires, baked cookies, and warm hugs.

'Here let me get that,' Eden grabbed the box off of him and placed it on the counter.

'Thank you my dear,' he replied and smiled from under his frail face.

'New records clearly,' Eden rummaged through the box of drenched records, excited to see what people had given up. She pulled out an ABBA one and wiped it dry. 'Who'd want to get rid of ABBA?' She laughed as she emptied out the box even further.

'There's a new artist in there somewhere. Archer…' He paused as he tried to think of the person on the album.

'Archer King,' Eden murmured.

'Yes, yes that's the one. Heard of him?' Mr Shore asked. Obviously Eden had heard of him.

'I have.' She smiled and went rummaging for the record. Mr Shore left for the small office in the shop, leaving Eden in there alone. She pulled out a navy blue record with white stars in the background. The outline of a man was drawn onto the front in a rough sort of sketch. Eden traced her fingers around the outline. She closed her eyes, and when she opened them again, a tear ran down her cheek. She remembered him again.

Junior year. First day of school. Eden had a free period before her first lesson of the day. She nearly always spent them in the music room, sitting by the piano. She had played it for as long as she could remember. There was something about it that made her fall in love with music all over again whenever she played it. Summer was just closing in on itself, but the sun still shone brightly in through the large window and reflected back from the piano's surface. There weren't many people that chose to spend their frees in the music room, they mostly smoked in the toilets or were bunking off school until they really had to come in.
There were an array of posters strung up on the walls surrounding her. Different productions the school had put on, old school bands, composers. The list went on. Nothing really truly succeeded in the school No one went on to do great things, not yet at least. It was a small high school situated in the middle of Iowa, the middle of nowhere. They had nothing to boost their dreams, apart from a terrible school headmaster who cancelled the school productions and made everyone drop any hopes and dreams they had. He always used to say that people born in Iowa never leave Iowa. That was true in some cases. Everyone who had gone to that school Eden had known either came back to work in the school, or to pursue their dreams of being a country writer in their Iowa ranch with all the animals.

The door opened. Eden swung round from where she was sitting at the piano.

'Oh sorry,' the boy said and went to close the door behind him and leave.

'No it's okay. Come in,' she ushered him inside. He was tall and strangely handsome, and Eden had never seen him before. She was always intrigued by new people who had the courage to transfer schools.

'I can leave, if you're busy,' he said again, pointing back to the door he had just entered.

'No, stay, it's nice to have company,' Eden replied.

The boy wore mostly all black, black jeans, a black t-shirt, and paired with black combat boots that looked too heavy to be wearing on his feet. Apart from that, he had a faded mustard yellow jacket on, more like a scottish tartan print that had been thrown onto a denim jacket. It looked like he was being forced to wear it, to make it look like he wasn't severely depressed by wearing the colour of death.

'I'm Eden,' she held out her hand, he shook it cautiously.

'Archie,' he smiled, before adding, 'Kingston.'

'Archie Kingston, welcome to hell,' Eden smiled and laughed a little.

He had overly dark hair to coincide with his dark attire. It hung in neat curls in front of his eyes which he occasionally swept to the side to reveal them. She felt drawn to them, the icy blue energy that was generated from them drew her in like she was being pulled into a whirlpool of emotion. She could read them. He was nervous. He fiddled with his hands, weaving his fingers in and out of each other like he was weaving thread.

'First day?' She asked him as he pulled up a chair next to the piano.
He nodded and looked at her, again with the mystical eyes.
'I can tell. Don't be nervous, it's just school, it'll be over before we know it.' She explained as she looked through the stack of sheet music she had placed in front of her previously.
'Do you play?' He asked and pointed to the piano.
'This? Yeah, I have all my life. Do you?' She asked back at him, brushing her fingers over the keys and desperately holding back from playing them.
'I've tried to teach myself, it never works though. I play guitar, and I sing,' he added. He had stopped playing with his hands and his knees had stopped bouncing up and down. The nerves seemed to be fading away, just as they should. A silence shadowed them, it wasn't awkward, just quiet.
'So, where did you come from?' Eden suddenly asked, to end the silence mainly.
'My mom's got a new job in the town, we originally came from Ohio, so not too far away,' he explained.
'Cool,' she nodded and smiled directly into his eyes. They spent their first period in the music room, no one interrupted them, which was unusual to Eden, usually someone wandered into the room, either lost, drunk, or both. This was a small high school in Iowa, not the Met Gala. Eden found out lots about Archie that day. He didn't have any siblings, he wanted to be a musician, and he released a song last year, but it never went viral. At least

he tried, she thought, you never get anywhere without trying.

Eden stuffed the record back into the box and picked it up so that she could organise them into their correct places. Fleetwood Mac, The Beatles, Nirvana, Led Zeppelin, more David Bowie. What was it about David Bowie that made everyone want to get rid of his albums? They were part of the culture they lived in, she thought. She made her way through the box, walking back and forth across the room slotting them into their correct places. Until, that is, she was left with one last one. Archer King.
'Hey Shore! Can I take this one home with me?' She shouted across the store hoping he would hear her. He came out from his small hiding and looked at what she was holding.
'Sure, I hope you enjoy it.' He gave her the thumbs up. She smiled at him as he left to go back into hibernation. She held the record in her hands. Archer King. She turned it around to read the back, the contents of the album. Of course she knew all the songs, apart from one. Eden placed it in her bag which she kept under the counter. Various thoughts raced through her mind. That album was dedicated to her, and no one knew. Archer hadn't told anyone who he had made that album for. About first love, first time happiness, and then, first heartbreak. Eden hoped that maybe, just maybe, her first love could be her last, and only love. Eden walked home after her shift had finished, holding tightly onto her bag which had encased in it, the record. The cold winter day had erupted onto the

city, she could feel the rain on her face, without it even falling. It was damp, and cold, and made the whole city feel low.

Juliet wasn't back yet. She was still at class. The apartment was as she had left it that morning, somewhat tidy, somewhat messy. The dishes were still stacked in the sink, she should probably clear them away before their guest arrived later. Eden didn't think twice before pulling out the old record player she brought everywhere with her. Before she had got the bed she had kept it in an empty kitchen cupboard, but now it was under her bed. She blew off the dust it had gathered, it wasn't much, but the feeling of blowing off dust always gave you that sense of you're doing something highly illegal and exciting. She pulled out the record from her bag and traced the outline of the boy on it, Archer King, America's new rock god extraordinaire. There was a crackling rustle before the first song played. Eden sat back on her bed and let the music escape into her ears. It was just a guitar, he was picking at the strings, making music that she had never thought would be successful. Eden closed her eyes, she could remember the day he first played that song to her.

She could picture him standing there in that music room where they met, one month after they first met. He wore the same outfit he always wore, the only thing he changed was his jacket. Every now and then he'd come into school wearing a new jacket. It was like his mom went shopping and brought back something new, a jacket, and she forced him to wear it to school until she came home a few weeks later with something new. The amount of jackets he had in his closet would be unbelievable. Eden sat there, watching Archie, as he was back then, picking at the strings on the guitar. His knuckles didn't shake like when she first met him, they were strong and tightly clasped together with the fingers slightly pointing out to delicately touch the guitar strings. The music he played was soft. She listened to every word, every beat in the music. He had written this, from his own pure heart, Archie had written this piece of music all by himself. He finished the song and swung his guitar back onto his back. Eden stood up from the stool she was sitting on and walked over to Archie.

'That, that was beautiful,' she said looking into his eyes. 'What's it called?' You could see the curiousness in her eyes, in her expression.

'The Brightest. Because you are the brightest star I know,' he looked back into her eyes before pulling her in closer to her. He wrapped his arms around her waist and she wrapped hers around his neck. Their foreheads touched. She could feel his warm breath against her face. They hesitated for a moment, looking into eachothers deep eyes. Warmth radiated through her body as his lips touched hers, she could feel his energy, his passion. He kissed her. He tasted like a crisp October morning, fresh coffee and leaves crunching on the floor, cold but with a little hint of warmth. As they parted she saw his lips curl into a rare smile, and she couldn't help but smile back.

Four

Eden knew when to hide everything. She received a text from Juliet saying she was ten minutes away. The album she hid in the draws beside her fold out bed and the record player she stuffed back under the metal frame. Eden kept playing that first song in her head. She lay back and rested her head against the wall behind her, clutching tight of the soft pillow. The Brightest. Was she really the brightest star? She felt as if suddenly the star had died, she had died, a supernova. There he was, Archer King, touring the country singing this song written for her, and now he sang it without feeling anything. What was the point in that? His love had hit her so hard and suddenly it was gone.
'What are you doing?'
Eden jumped up from where she was, it was Juliet. She must've dozed off whilst sitting there.
'Just thinking,' Eden said quietly, almost too quiet for Juliet to hear.

'You haven't taken anything have you?' Juliet asked jokingly. Eden gave her a hard stare. 'Okay not funny, sorry.' Juliet took off her coat and placed it on the hook next to the door. A boy walked through the door. This must be Jason, she thought.

'Right get up, make yourself presentable,' Juliet told Eden. Eden prised the duvet off from over her body and swung her legs around to stand up. What was Juliet on about? She looked perfectly presentable. Her faded black jeans hung loosely around her hips and her jumper, despite being slightly oversized, looked fine.

'Hi, I'm Jason,' Jason walked around Juliet and held out his hand. Eden hesitated a moment before taking it and smiling. His hand was cold and dry, she could feel the skin cracking and his fingers were long and boney.

'I know, Juliet always talks about you,' Eden replied, knowing Juliet would flush a shade of rosy pink. In return, Juliet too gave Eden a hard stare and mouthed something that Eden could make out, but chose to ignore. Jason turned around to look at Juliet who stood there and waved, before sticking her middle finger up at Eden and storming into the kitchen.

'This is a nice place you've got,' Jason exclaimed as he walked around, getting a feel for it.

'Juliet's parents are loaded, that's why,' Eden told him.

The rest of the evening went like this:

Juliet made spaghetti bolognese, Eden found it ironic how she had invited her assumed crush over and made him the most romantic meal she could think of. Eden felt like she was third wheeling in a way. They played the only

board game they could find in the apartment, that stupid game of life game where you live out a life on the board. Anything would be better than this life, Eden thought. At least this way she could have some control over it all.
They were laughing and touching each other. Eden just looked at them from the other side of the table in disgust. Eden was afraid that Juliet would fall in love with Jason and then it would all be over and she would head down the same path as Eden. She didn't want anyone to feel the pain she felt, because it was unbearable.
'So Eden,' Jason started as they had just sat down at the sofas, 'what are you up to? Like, what do you do?' he asked.
Eden gulped, she could tell the truth, but then, had Juliet already told him everything about her.
'I work at the record shop down the road, just part time, to fill the time. I was thinking of applying for NYU's music programme for this September too.' She explained as she took a sip of the hot chocolate she had made.
'You play music?' He questioned.
Eden nodded, 'yeah, piano mainly. I was taught guitar, um... two years ago as well.' There was hesitation as she spoke. Archie had taught her guitar. She hadn't picked it up since it all happened just before Christmas. It lay under her bed by the record player she had hidden.
'That's so cool. I played drums in a high school band of mine,' Jason replied smiling. 'Yeah we were called the The Four J's, because all four of us had names beginning with J. I cringe back on it now.'

Eden could see why Juliet liked Jason. He was funny, he liked to talk, a lot, and he seemed like he cared a lot for his friends. If anything, she didn't mind if she saw more of Jason, just as long as he didn't break Juliet's heart.

'So, what was Juliet like back in high school?' Jason asked again. This guy liked to ask questions Eden thought. She put down her mug on the table in front of her and pulled the blanket up over her knees.

'Well, she's been my best friend for as long as I remember. She was this really book nerdy kid who always had her nose in a book, even when walking down corridors. People used to bump into her on purpose,' Eden explained. Juliet looked down at the floor, like she was embarrassed. There wasn't anything to be embarrassed about, Eden found it unique.

'And she was smart, but not too smart to be classed as a nerd. She played football as well, I bet you didn't know that,' Eden laughed. It was always a funny sight when Juliet came off of the pitch covered in mud on a rainy November afternoon. Eden had always gone to most of her matches, if she could make them, or if she wasn't making out with Archie in the music room that was. A memory of that flashed before Eden's eyes. Her face sank and you could tell something she didn't like the idea of had come across her.

'Eden, you okay?' Juliet asked as she moved to sit by her.

'Yes, yes I am. Sorry.' She faked a smile, but really she wasn't okay.

'Well, maybe I'll challenge you to a game of football one day,' Jason said to break the silence.

'Oh you wouldn't dare. I'd absolutely thrash you, ten to one.'
The three of them laughed, although Eden didn't laugh properly. She just went along with them. That's what she did most days. She pretended like everything was okay, when really, she was just as bad as before, she just didn't show it. Maybe that was what she was doing wrong. Maybe all she had to do was become an ace pretender and everyone would treat her normally like she wasn't mentally depressed.
Jason left just before ten, he didn't live far away, he said. And then it was just two of them, again. They cleared away the plates they had left at the table from dinner and removed the mugs that had piled up on the coffee table by the sofa. Juliet turned the radio on that sat just next to the old rusty toaster that on most occasions, was broken.
'...coming up we have Archer King, the nineteen year old rock sensation that is America's favourite new artist of our decade. His first album, also called *Firsts*, has skyrocketed all the way to number one, but for now, here is his new single, *Strangers Always You*.' The radio turned to playing the song. Eden stood there holding the dirty dishes. She didn't say anything.
'We can turn it off if you want,' Juliet said. She had moved to face Eden who was staring at the radio.
'No, I want to hear it.'
They stood there in silence listening to the song playing from the radio. Eden let the music flow into her ears, the lyrics were raw and real. This song wasn't on the album she realised, it was new. There were moments in the song

where she could picture Archie in the studio singing it, tears slowly falling down his face. He was playing his guitar, but like it was the only thing he could do. There were mistakes in his playing, he played the wrong note, the wrong chord, it didn't sound put together, and yet it sounded perfect. Music was his therapy, it helped him get through everything. If he was upset, he turned to music, he wrote music as a way to end the suffering. But the suffering never ended. Not for Eden at least.

She left the kitchen in silence and sat on her bed, knees tightly pressed to her chest. Juliet eventually followed her in after contemplating whether she should let Eden be alone for the rest of the night.

'Do you like him?' Eden asked as Juliet perched on the end of the bed.

'Who? Archer?' She replied, knowing that she meant Jason, but didn't want to say it.

'No, Jason. Do you like him?' Eden asked again. Tears rolled down from her face. She spoke in a quiet hushed voice just loud enough for Juliet to hear her. She had brushed her long hair behind her ears and her eyes had returned to their red puffy state they used to be.

'Of course I like Jason. He's my friend.' Juliet held out her hand for Eden to take. She let it sink into the white sheets before Eden took it. They smiled, or at least Juliet smiled.

'Do you love him?' Eden then asked.

Juliet sat there, still holding onto Eden's cold hand and rocked back and forth. She brought her legs up onto the bed and crossed them so she was looking straight at Eden.

'I don't know,' Juliet finally said. There was a pause in their short conversation. 'Tell me about him.'
'Who?'
'Archer. Talk to me about him. I'm sure there are things even you kept from me.' Juliet suggested.
Eden tried to think of a specific moment in time where she and Archer had been more than just a happy couple.
'After we started dating, Archie would take me to these places he had googled. He was new to the area, but these places he took me to were new to me. Clearly I hadn't explored the vacant Iowa town that we lived in enough,' Eden started to say. She chuckled for a tenth of a second. 'But there was one place that I remember vividly. Archie took me to this park with a lake November of junior year. It was dark, we went there because apparently it has the best sights for stargazing, although usually it's good everywhere because the skies are so vast and huge. He brought us blankets and we set them out on the banks of the lake and watched the stars. Nothing really happened, but it was the conversation that I think stuck with me.
He told me he loved me that night. He told me he wanted to marry me and grow old. We were only sixteen, and yet I told him that I loved him and I wanted to marry him. He gave me this pebble as an engagement ring, he hadn't prepared to propose.'
Eden pulled out a small pebble from a box that sat on the bedside table. It had sharp rough edges, it wasn't smooth like most of the pebbles you see on shore. If anything, it was a rock.

'You were… engaged?' Juliet asked, shocked. You could see it in her expression.

'Surprise.' Eden smiled and presented jazz hands.

'Did you ever tell your parents?' Juliet was full of questions. This was new information to her. She didn't want to leave anything out.

'Do you think my parents would approve of their sixteen year old daughter marrying her boyfriend of one month?' Eden had cheered up, not much, but it was enough to put a small smile on her face which had so often been drowned in tears.

'We thought that if we made the promise to marry each other then nothing would tear us apart. Because he told me that he always kept in his promises. That's what I loved about him,' Eden explained. 'We had planned a life together, to marry, buy a tiny beach house in California, have two kids, one boy and one girl, grow old together.'

'But everything comes to an end,' Juliet answered.

'That's what I was so afraid of,' she replied.

Juliet left Eden after a while. When she could tell she was gone, Eden pulled out the album from under her bed and looked at it again. Each time she brushed her fingers over the outline of Archie a pulse of energy ran through her veins. The second song on the album was called Mercury. She was drawn back to the lake, that night he proposed to her.

They lay there gazing up at night sky, their fingers tightly woven together.

'You see that,' Archie pointed up to the sky with his free hand, 'that's Mercury.'
'Where?' Eden asked as she tilted her head towards Archie and tried to figure out where he was pointing.
'Here,' he reached across her body and took her hand, and then guided her pointed finger to where Mercury was.
'It's beautiful,' she exclaimed. She let out a heavy breath.
'The brightest in the sky tonight,' he added. They looked at each other. His eyes were almost as dark as the night sky. He cupped his hand around her ear and kissed her. She didn't want to stop kissing him. Everything in that moment right then seemed unimportant. Everything but him. He was her whole world, she knew she loved him there and then. He kissed her gently, but it wasn't the gentleness she wanted. She wanted everything, all of him. She traced her fingers down his neck in circles and smiled as he pressed her lips firmer onto hers.
'Don't stop,' she whispered, and so he didn't.

Eden woke up the next morning still clutching the record. She had run her mascara crying herself to sleep. There was sunlight bursting through the window for a change, she could feel the warmth as it hit her toes that poked out from out of the covers.
'Eden I'm leaving, I'll be back just after lunch.' she heard Juliet call and then the door shut quietly.
She lay there with the album still tightly wrapped under her arms before getting up, washed and dressed. The radio played quietly in the background as she made her breakfast and sat at the table ready to open the

newspaper that had been delivered that morning. He was everywhere, in the newspaper, on the radio, hidden under her bed. Eden couldn't get him out of her mind. She hadn't been able to for months now. Maybe the problem was that she hadn't tried to let go. Maybe she didn't want to let go of him.

Five

Christmas Eve. Junior year. The middle of a field in Iowa. Snow, and lot's of it.
'Why are we out here?' Eden asked as she took big steps over the snow which came up to almost her knees.
'You'll have to wait and see,' Archie answered, taking Eden's hand that had almost frozen from the cold surrounding them. The field was untouched. It was covered in a thick blanket of snow that had settled neatly on the earth. Gentle and still. Cold to touch. And beautiful in all of it's fine glory.
'Almost there,' Archie said as they waded through the wave of snow.
Eden shivered in the cold and dug her chin into the scarf she had so neatly wrapped around her neck. Archie had given it to her only the week before when they had visited a Christmas market together and bought each other funny gifts. Eden had bought him the ugliest Christmas jumper that he had promised to wear on Christmas Day, but she didn't believe him. And the scarf which she had on was

decorated with brussel sprouts dressed up as Santas and elves and Christmas puddings.

'Okay then,' he announced and threw his hands up in the air, 'we're here!'

They had come to the top of a hill, which overlooked what seemed to look like an army of snowmen. All different shapes and sizes.

'Oh my goodness,' Eden exclaimed as she took in the sights. There had to be at least one hundred of them. Huge piles of snow were dotted around on the outskirts, presumably for making more.

'I thought we'd make a snowman to add to the armada that people have already made,' Archie explained. He took her hand and led her down the hill. The snow there was sparse, it had been collected and added to the mountains of snow on the sides.

'What gave you this idea?' She asked and laughed as he pulled her arm in the direction of the entrance.

'Well every year people donate hats and scarfs apparently, and the money they raise goes towards helping those who can't afford Christmas meals and presents and stuff like that. Besides, who doesn't love building a snowman?' He added. Eden stopped halfway down the hill and brought her cold hands up to his cheek. He shivered as their skin touched.

'I love it. I love you. I love that you put other people's needs before yours,' she said. He took hold of her hand on his cheek.

'I love you too,' he returned before pressing his lips against hers. Snow started to fall from the sky. It landed on Eden's eyelashes and her nose. He wiped them away as they parted.

'Come on, let's go build a snowman.' He took her hand and they ran down the hill.

Eden watched Archie as he lifted the head of their snowman onto the slightly distorted body they had shaped. The scarf they had collected was an old mustard yellow one that had the smell of an old person. They wrapped it around and placed the stones in to make small buttons down the front of what looked like a slightly odd snowman.

'What shall we call it?' Archie asked as Eden rested her head on his shoulder and wrapped her arms around his warm body.

'Joe Cocker,' Eden said after a few moments of thinking.

'Any reason behind that wonderful name?' He asked, kissing the top of her head which had now been covered in small, but beautiful snowflakes.

'You are so beautiful. That's why.' She looked up at his face which had a light glisten to it as he smiled his broad smile he always did when he was happy. She kissed him quickly and then pulled out her phone to take a photo of Archie and Joe Cocker. He knelt down into the snow and hugged the snowman, but gently so that it didn't crumble under the weight of his arms. They then switched so that Eden got a picture. Her cheeks had gone a shade of red as she knelt down and smiled at the camera.

'You kids want me to take a photo?' A man, covered head to toe in one of those skiing onesies coloured grey walked up from behind them and pointed at Eden's camera. Archie and Eden looked at each other and shrugged.

'That would be amazing thanks,' Eden answered and Archie passed the camera to him. The two of them knelt either side of Joe Cocker and smiled. It looked like a family portrait those big expensive families hung up in their gigantic hallway of dead people.

'I hope Joe Cocker has a nice life,' Eden said as they walked back up the hill the way they had come from.

'I'm sure he'll have a great life, just look at all of his friends.' Archie pointed to all of the other snowmen mysterious people had made over the days the project had been open.

'His parents will always love him,' she replied and placed her hand in his.

'Forever.'

They got back into town just before six. Archie pulled up outside Eden's house so she could get out. It was dark now, it had been for a few hours now.

'I wanted to give you this, as a Christmas present.' He pulled out a small box from the car door. It was wrapped in red paper and had a brown paper tag attached to it. She looked up into his eyes before taking hold of the box and unwrapping it carefully. Beneath the paper was a green velvet box with a gold coloured strip across the middle. She opened the box cautiously and looked inside. Gasp. It was the most gorgeous, most beautiful ring she had ever laid eyes on. A single gold band with a white diamond attached to it.

'How... how did you buy this?' She managed to say between breaths.

'I sold a guitar and some other things, plus one of my songs made some cash so I put it all towards it,' he explained, 'but it was all worth it.' He cupped his hand around her ear and pulled her in to kiss her. Still holding on to the box she wrapped her arms around his neck and leant over the gear stick. His warm breath met hers. This was forever, she thought as she pulled him in closer and kissed him longer. This was cosmic love, love like no other. He was unique, she had never met anyone like this before. They shared the same passion for everyone and everything. They shared the same passion for each other. The street was empty and deserted. Eden's house looked quiet. She led him upstairs into her bedroom and locked the door tightly behind her.

'Merry Christmas,' he whispered as he lay her down on the bed and slowly undid the sweet blue shirt she was wearing. In the dimly lit room their fingers caressed the others skin like anything heavier would destroy it. In the moment it was just them against everything else. They became one, mad with love for the other. Their bodies fit perfectly together. Archie ran his fingers up her toned thigh, she clung on to his shoulders tightly and let him kiss her even more.

And then they fell asleep under her covers gazing into each others eyes, their arms wrapped around the other, holding on for dear life.

'I should probably go,' Archie whispered into her ear. He pressed his lips against hers and pulled the covers away from him. Eden watched him put his clothes back on. His figure was tall and handsome. He leant in and kissed her again and then smiled.

'I love you,' he said.

'I love you too,' she took his hand as he walked out of the room, until it dropped by her side yet again.

You Are So Beautiful. That was the next song on the album. Archie had done a cover to it. The third song.

Six

'And what's your name dear?' Camille asked. Eden had found herself sitting in one of those luminous, stereotypical circles surrounded by people with actual diagnosed illnesses. The *Here to Help* support group met in a large room with colourful pictures decorating the walls. Clearly they tried to make it seem welcoming when really it was just a bunch of people who were too scared to talk to the people they live with so instead they talked to strangers. Eden could feel all eyes on her. She was being drowned in stares from all angles of the room. Her knuckles clenched together and she dug her nails into the sweaty palms of her hand. Already they had started to form crescent moons delicately placed there.
'I'm Eden, nineteen, not sure why I'm here to be honest. No illnesses that I've been diagnosed with. I guess I'm just constantly feeling unwanted, lost, trapped inside of this perfect bubble I've been living in for the past three years, and all of a sudden, the bubble has popped, but I haven't caught up yet. So I'm living in this bubble, without there actually being a bubble now. Do you understand? And

sometimes I feel like I've caught up and I'm free, and the other time I feel like there's a heavy weight on me that's just continuously dragging me back to the start. And I don't want to go back to the start. I can't rewind, I need to keep pushing forward, but I don't know how.' Eden stopped and stared at the ground. Everything she had just said didn't even make sense to her, so how would anyone else understand it?

Camille looked at her from across the room. She was the leader, the anchor, of the support group. She was dark skinned, and had short dark hair that stopped just above her shoulders. Her smile was wide and pretty, and she looked like she had just been dropped off by God from the sun to spread light and happiness.

'Thank you Eden. Perhaps when we've finished you'd like to talk about this further?' Camille asked and smiled sweetly. Eden nodded, but didn't say anything. She felt that she had done too much talking for one day. There were nine other people in the room, most of them around the same age as Eden.

'Hi my name's Loren, I'm twenty, and last year I tried to kill myself for the fourth time. I've struggled with anorexia since I was fifteen, I'm diagnosed bipolar and I have depression and anxiety. All my life I've been in and out of hospital, I've had moments when we thought I was getting much better, there were moments when we thought I was in my last few days. But here I am, barely scraping by, and I'm thankful every single day, because if I didn't survive, I wouldn't have experienced all the amazing things that have been thrown in my path,' Loren finished

saying and looked around the room. She was small, you could see the bone structure in her face. Her hair was blonde and freshly straightened, with a black headband crossing the top of her head. She also wore these big glasses which covered a large proportion of her face. Her clothes looked old and too big for her, like she had just gone to the shop and bought the first things she saw. She wore huge chunky Dr Martens which had clearly been previously owned. She bounced her knees up and down as she sat there, her hands fell between her legs, sitting there slightly hunched over.
'Thank you Loren, we're here for you.' Camille said, before the rest of the group agreed with her. The meeting went on for another thirty minutes, everyone sharing their stories and why they were sitting in the circle. Eden couldn't wait for it to end, she didn't even know why she decided to go in the first place.
Even here Eden felt like she didn't fit in. Everyone else seemed to have a story to tell, she just sat there and listened to them. The group ended at eleven, and Camille invited them to join her for coffee and cake that she had clearly bought from the nearest 7-Eleven. Some people left because they had 'important things' to attend. Eden thought it was just an excuse to leave because they couldn't cope with talking to anyone for much longer. There were roughly three groups of people dotted around the hall. Eden just stood by the cheap cake and took small sips from the incredibly weak coffee that was practically inedible.
'Eden right?' Loren walked up to her and smiled.

'Yes, you're Loren?' Eden asked. She wrapped both hands around the mug tightly. Talking to new people wasn't her strongest trait.

'I am, I heard you from across the room, you seem like a really nice person, and I'm really sorry for what you're going through right now, it must be hard,' Loren admitted. Immediately Eden felt like there was someone she could finally sympathise with, not that they shared anything in common, because they didn't, but it was nice to be able to talk to someone about it.

'Oh, yes, I mean, I'm surviving. But it's nothing to what you've been through,' Eden confessed.

'So what do you do for fun?' Loren asked. People who asked questions got on Eden's nerves, just a little bit.

'I work down at Shore's Records, just arranging and rearranging the shelves mainly, play piano from time to time, you know, I enjoy music. What about you?' Eden felt it was only fair to return the question.

'I read, a lot. I write too, lots of poetry,' she replied and nodded.

'Then you'll love my friend Juliet. Our whole apartment is filled to the brim with different books,' Eden laughed shyly and took and sip yet again from the diluted coffee.

'I'd like to meet her, it's not everyday you meet an avid book fanatic like me,' Loren exclaimed. 'What music do you listen to?' She asked again.

'Old music mainly. Bowie, ABBA, Whitney Houston. Queen too, they've been my recent obsession,' Eden replied.

'Love all of them. I played guitar a bit in high school, but was never very good at it, plus, I never got the time to play what with going in and out of hospital.' Loren seemed to always laugh whenever she mentioned the word hospital. Like it was a trigger to make her giggle or smile. She was coping, she could deal with her mind. Despite still not being perfect, Loren was able to grab hold of her life and change it when she felt herself going backwards. She could go forward now without any help.

'I've got to go, but it was nice talking to you, here's my number,' Loren wrote down her number on an unused napkin by the cake and pushed it into Eden's spare hand. 'I'll see you soon.' She grabbed her bag which was sitting on one of the chairs and walked out of the room.

Eden looked down at the napkin in her hand, the numbers were messy, and the ink from the pen had spread slightly across the paper. It didn't matter, she probably wouldn't even message her back.

The hall filed out of people until it left just two. Eden and Camille. All of a sudden the room turned a shade of cold and the windows started to display raindrops. Yet again, winter had shown its true colours.

'How are you feeling?' Camille asked as they sat down at chairs opposite each other. She had a strange, creepy type of smile that Eden didn't exactly like to look at, but felt she was obliged to.

'I'm fine, thank you. I spoke to Loren after, she seemed nice. We might meet up again sometime soon,' Eden replied quickly. It was most definitely, probably a lie. The less conversation the better she thought.

'That's good, I'm glad to see you're talking to people. It must be hard to be confused as to where you stand in this world, but I can assure you, you stand at an equal level to everyone. No one is above you, and no one is below you. In this world we are all equal. We always feel like we are constantly being dragged behind, but that's just the way of life. Now, tell me, is there a reason why you're feeling like this?' She questioned. Her voice was calming and soothing, it sounded like she had walked into a room to get a massage. Eden could picture the calming music playing in the background as she rested her head on the bed. She took time to process everything she had just heard. It didn't make sense. No one she knew before today had felt like they were being pulled back, they all seemed to be running the race too fast if anything.
Eden hesitated, there were very few people that knew the real story. And she wanted it to stay that way.
'Does everything I say stay confidential?' She wondered. Camille nodded,
'Everything we say here will stay between you and me.'
'There was a guy, we loved each other so dearly, and then one day he quit on me and left me hanging. I had been so wrapped up in his life that I had forgotten how to live my own, I feel like everyone else had learnt to live, and I was just picking up the pieces. He broke me, and I don't think it can be fixed.' Eden confessed. A tear had emerged from the corner of her eye which she quickly wiped away with the sleeve of her jumper.

'Was there a reason why it ended so suddenly?' Camille asked again. It was like she was trying to draw out the answers to this story that had been kept so secret before.
'We had a fight, I said some stuff, he said some stuff. He said that I loved him too much. I don't think you can ever love someone too much,' Eden sobbed as she looked up at Camille.
'So this person, would I recognise him?' Yet again another question. It was at this point Eden knew she could either lie, or tell the truth. She could tell Camille that she was Archer King's mysterious lover who 'broke his heart'. She took the easier option.
'No,' she shook her head, 'he was just obsessed with himself.' If anything, he was too obsessed with his career that he forgot to ever include Eden in it. Maybe he was embarrassed with Eden?
'I think to truly let go of this, you need to reach out to him. Tell him how you feel. Maybe then you'll get the answers you're looking for. The answers which he left pending.' Camille reached over and placed her hand on Eden's knee. 'I believe in you. You're just afraid to move on because you don't know how. I was once like you, young and in love, clearly it didn't work out, I mean look at me, I'm a divorced mother of four with the father off with some eighteen year old. And i'm doing just fine.'
Eden left Camille soon after and walked back to the apartment. She kept replaying what she had been told just minutes before. She needed to let go, and the only way she could do that was to get the answers from him, because only he had the answers.

The streets were strangely filled with people despite the heavens opening over New York City. Puddles had been trampled in by little children who were now covered in muddy rain water. Eden pulled out the napkin Loren had written her number on and typed it into her phone.

Hey it's Eden. It was so nice meeting you today, it felt good to be able to talk to someone. Why don't we meet up for coffee soon? - Eden X

She didn't expect Loren to reply so quickly, but in a matter of minutes her phone buzzed and presented a message.

Hi! Yes coffee sounds great, how about Friday @ 11am? The Coffee Crib, my treat. -L

Eden smiled as she read the message in her head.

Perfect, thank you. I'll see you then -Eden X

For the first time that day Eden had smiled properly, although it only lasted a short amount of time before her finger landed on Archie's contact details. She hadn't deleted them, not yet. Eden had always thought he would reach out to her, apologise, want to make amends, but it had never happened. And by now Eden had accepted that he would never reach out to her, she would have to reach out to him.

Eden pressed delete, her thumb hovered over the confirm button. She read and reread the last message she had ever sent him, and then deleted his number. But nothing changed, and she loved him more than ever.

Eden got home in time for lunch. Juliet was in the kitchen singing to herself.

'Hey,' Eden called out as she dumped her coat on the floor and took her shoes off.

'Hey how was it?' was her reply. Eden walked into the kitchen and pulled out a chair.
'Yeah it was fine, lots of depressed people talking about their feelings,' she admitted.
'So you fit in just perfectly then?' Juliet jokingly replied, before adding, 'that was a joke.'
Eden had learnt to deal with Juliet's strange comments about depression.
'So what's for lunch?' Eden managed to say to change the topic. She stood up from the chair and looked over into the saucepan.
'Pasta, I was really craving it,' Juliet laughed and continued to stir the contents.
'Pregnancy cravings more like?' Eden said sarcastically. Juliet gave her a hard glare.
'Jason and I are just friends, nothing romantic going on there.'
'Right then… friends,' Eden replied. The two of them laughed and served up the uncooked pasta which Juliet had made. She was known for not being the best of cooks, but at least she tried.
'I'm meeting Jason later, so you'll have the place to yourself for the afternoon,' Juliet said as they ate lunch.
'Friends…' Eden repeated and laughed, accidentally missing her mouth and letting the food fall onto her lap. Juliet kicked Eden from the table.
She left soon after, leaving Eden alone. Eden spread her legs across the sofa and pulled out her phone. She flicked through the photos of her and Archie, she had deleted them yet, maybe she would never delete them. Eden

threw her phone onto her bed, it bounced and then relaxed on her pillow. She pulled out the dusty guitar which hadn't been played in months and sat back down on the sofa, tuning the strings until it sounded playable. Her fingers brushed against the strings and she rested her chin on the body of the guitar.

She started to lighty play the instrument. It was rusty, there were mistakes, yet she played. Her voice quivered as she sang the lyrics. The fourth song on the album. Eden had written this song January of junior year. She hadn't heard, or sung it in what seemed like years, but it came naturally to her. The lyrics flowed out of her mouth and into the air around her. She pictured herself sitting on her bed back in Iowa, Archie crossed legged in front of her hearing the song for the first time. The guitar was new to her back then, she knew but a few chords, but the ones she did created such beauty in her music that she didn't need to know any others. The song was nothing but poetry played against music, it was messy and broken, but that's what made it so perfect to Archie. He tilted his head as he let the lyrics seep into his brain and dig holes in his scalp. They were cemented in him.
She opened her eyes and realised it was all just a memory. The guitar she had bought from Ebay lay on her lap, she had stopped playing. It had happened again. She had let the past take over her mind and allude her into thinking she was happy again. Eden got up and reached for the hidden record under her bed. She ran her fingers down it until it landed on track number four. *Follow My*

Voice. That was her song. Without thinking she pulled out her record player and heaved it up onto her bed. She placed the vinyl neatly into place and carefully skipped the first three songs. She needed to hear his voice singing her words. For a moment she didn't think it would play, and then she heard the same three chords she had played minutes before. He hadn't changed anything, the lyrics were exactly the same. The music was the same. Eden didn't know how to react, her song had made it onto a best selling album, and everyone thought Archie had written it. She let the song play out before putting everything back where it had come from. Her mind raced back to the day she had written that song. One part of it jumped out over any other part:

   You know you can follow my voice
    If you've got no other choice
    From you heart to your brain
     Know that I'm yours

Except, she wasn't his, and he wasn't hers. They were two people trying to run away from each other. The song didn't make any sense now.

Seven

On Friday morning, Juliet baked fresh chocolate chip cookies and read the newspaper she had got up so early to get. She cleaned the kitchen down, and then the living room, turning on the vacuum cleaner and moving it across the floor. She hummed to herself as she moved her arm back and forth, cleaning the apartment down finally. She thought about Eden, it was the only thing she could think of recently. What if she did it again? And what if she didn't get there in time? Juliet dropped to her knees and pushed the vacuum under Eden's bed to pick up the dust and muck that had collected there over the past few weeks. She switched the vacuum off suddenly and reached under, curious as to why there was hardly any space under there. Her hand fumbled under the bed, pulling out various items of clothing and boxes of stuff that Eden had acquired until she came across a flat cardboard case. Juliet pulled it out and brushed off the dust that sat on top of it. She squinted in the sunlight and read what was on it. Before even finishing reading it she knew what it was. And to be totally honest, she wasn't surprised either.

Juliet heard the shower stop and the bathroom door open. Eden walked out, towel wrapped around her, humming quietly to herself. She saw Juliet sitting on her bed staring down at the album she had so carefully hidden under her bed.

'So what are we now, snooping around my stuff?' Eden grabbed the album from Juliet's hands and held her towel firm around her body.

'I thought we had put all of this behind us,' Juliet replied and stood up to face Eden.

'Oh my god Juliet, give a girl some privacy. I don't go looking around your room,' Eden exclaimed.

'I wasn't snooping, I promise. I just came across it.'

Eden picked up the clothes she had laid on her bed before she got in the shower. She couldn't hide anything, she realised. Juliet will always, one way or another, be a part of this.

'Why do you even have it anyway?' Juliet asked and pointed to the album tucked under Eden's arm.

'Why do you even care?' Eden rolled her eyes and turned her back to Juliet.

'Because I'm trying to look out for you Eden. This person destroyed you once already, I won't let him destroy you again.' Her voice was raised and her cheeks had gone a shade of red.

'That's not your decision to make,' was all Eden replied with.

'Actually... yeah it is. You tried to kill yourself a few weeks ago because of him. What if you do that again, but this time, you don't survive?' Juliet said angrily.

'You know sometimes I wish I did die that day,' Eden admitted. A tear had appeared in the corner of her eye which she quickly wiped away. She wouldn't cry about this, she had promised herself.
'You don't mean that,' Juliet shook her head and tried to walk towards Eden.
'Get away from me,' Eden retracted back from Juliet in disgust. She was breathing heavily and quickly. You could see her heart beating up and down in her chest.
'Let me help,' Juliet said, 'please.'
'I don't need your help.' Eden continued to step backwards holding the album in one hand and her clothes in the other. She didn't take her eyes off Juliet, her skin formed tiny little mountains where there were goosebumps and she could feel a chill run all the way down her spine.
'Please just leave me alone,' Eden cried out and wiped the tears from her eyes.
'I can't do that, please let me help,' Juliet pleaded. Her voice was calming and smooth. But there was fear in her eyes, she stretched her arms out towards Eden, desperate to help. She was scared. Eden was fragile and needed mending, and fast.
'I can't do this,' Eden whispered and fell to the ground, dropping everything that she had acquired in her arms. Juliet rushed to her side and cradled her in her arms. Her hair was wet against Juliet's freshly dried clothes, but it didn't matter. Eden felt the last thread that had been keeping her going fray and break. She was tipped over, plummeting down into an endless pit of darkness.

Distraught sobs shook her broken body as she buried her head into Juliet. She tried to fight back, claiming control over the darkness that had hit her, but she lost. For the first time, Eden had lost, and she couldn't win.
'I can't do this,' Eden managed to say again over the crying and tears.
'Yes you can,' Juliet stroken the top of Eden's hair and kissed it softly. Eden tried to wipe away the continuous stream of tears which had now drowned her face.
'I'm done.' Eden whispered.
'No you're not. You're only just beginning,' Juliet replied and sat Eden up so that they were both cross legged on the floor of the kitchen. 'Talk to me.'
Eden heaved a big sigh and danced her fingers along the tiles of the kitchen floor.
'It's like having something that was a part of you ripped out. We were soulmates. We were meant to be together before the world was even made. We were put in this world to be together and it's like we've broken the rules of the universe by not being together. And I'm being punished, not him. Me. I want to be able to fucking live again, and not think about him. We were preassigned, designed in the stars, so why is he not here? You don't know how much I would give to be able to talk to him,' Eden tried to say through the tears and sobs. She had been crying like her brains on the inside were being shredded and torn. Her words were intertwined with each other and her sentences were messy through the frequent short breaths that she took.
'Maybe you should do just that,' Juliet said.

'Do what?' Eden looked at her confused.
'Talk to him. Maybe he feels the exact same,' she suggested.
'You know I can't do that.' Eden shook her head and looked down at the floor. She tried to make out a vague smile, as if she was mocking what Juliet had just said.
'How else are you supposed to get over him?' Juliet asked.
Eden shrugged and moved her fingers across the floor. She closed her eyes and rested her head on Juliet's lap. Maybe thinking about him would ease the pain- just slightly.

The last day of January, junior year. The music room had become like a safe sanctuary where Eden and Archie could spend time together during the school hours. They had made it their own. Eden's fingers moved quickly as she typed the long, but important essay her English teacher had set her over the weekend, that surprise, she hadn't completed. It was due in for the last period, she would have time. She hadn't seen Archie for most of the day, he hadn't even texted her. Eden missed his adorable curly hair, and his bright blue eyes that lit up when he saw her. The clock ticked by, she glanced up at it, because maybe, just maybe, he would come and find her.
'You'll never guess what...' Archie came into the room and set his bag down on the table opposite the piano. He was smiling, a smile that Eden had never seen before, something had happened.

'Hey Eden, how are you? Sorry I haven't texted you, or seen you today for that matter,' Eden said sarcastically and closed the lid on her laptop.

'Sorry, but I'll show you why now.' He squatted so he was head level with Eden and pulled her in for a kiss. She didn't kiss him back. Archie looked at her confused. There was worry in his eyes, something that had just appeared.

'Are you mad at me?' He asked.

Eden gulped. She wasn't mad, she could never be mad at Archie. She was just slightly, but also very, annoyed at the fact that he hadn't even bothered to reach out to her today.

'I haven't seen you all day. You didn't text me, what if something bad had happened?' Eden stood up from her chair and walked away from him. He followed, immediately.

'Well I'm sorry if you thought I was dead, but I have a reason.' He opened his bag and pulled out a black folder filled with papers.

'There always is a reason,' Eden replied angrily.

'Well I won't show you if you're not interested,' Archie flung the file onto the table where he had picked it up. Some of the papers scattered over the surface and fell by her feet, she knelt down and picked them up carelessly, piling them back on the table and folding her arms to look at Archie. Eden's face was flushed and hot, which juxtaposed Archie's cooler outlook.

'Archie we're supposed to be in this together. You can't just go off the face of the earth for a few hours and not tell me,' she spoke. Her voice was harsh, yet it quivered.

He stepped back a few paces and looked at her, scowling. 'You really want to know why I was out? Do you really want to know?' He snapped and pointed at her like he was ratting her out.

'Yes, I do,' she almost yelled, but it was quieter than she expected.

'Fine.' He thrust the papers from the file in her face. She took them from him and glanced down, scanning the writing. 'I was going to surprise you later today, but I guess I'll just show you here before you storm out of the room.'

Eden read what was in her hands. Contracts.

'I signed with a record label, thought I'd bring you to the studio to surprise you, but clearly that's not happening now.' He gathered up his belongings and stormed out of the room leaving Eden standing there in the middle. A tear rolled down from her eye. Their first fight.

It wasn't that he hadn't spoken to her that made her angry she realised later that day. For years Eden had dreamt of becoming a musician, signing a label with a company so that she could showcase her music. She was jealous. And jealousy had led her into becoming angry, and she was pretty sure Archie knew that.

Eden didn't stay behind after school for anything, she went back home and flung herself onto her bed. There was no telling how long she lay there for. No matter how hard she tried to stop herself, the fight just replayed in her mind, it was like it was haunting her, telling her she was in the wrong. Which she was. But she didn't want to accept it.

There was a faint knock on the door. It opened. Eden heaved herself to turn around to see who had entered.
'Can I come in?' Archie stood in the doorway. His hair was messier than usual and his eyes didn't give off their natural glow.
Eden rolled over onto one side of the bed and let Archie have the other side. She patted the sheets down as he took his shoes off and lay on the bed, looking deeply into her eyes.
'I'm sorry,' he whispered as he tucked a loose piece of Eden's hair behind her ear.
'Arch, it's okay,' she barely said. More tears rolled down from her face. Archie wiped them away for her, he couldn't bare to see his whole world cry. It made him want to cry.
'No it's not okay. I shouldn't have been so pissed off that you were worried about me just because I didn't call you.' He ran his fingers through her blonde hair like they were pieces of silk and gold.
'I'm so proud of you, you deserve it. I'm just trying to wrap my head around the fact that you're signed, you got your dream,' she smiled vaguely and sighed.
'I love you, I really hate it when we fight,' he said softly. He was apologising for something that he didn't even do wrong. He was a hopeless romantic that only wanted to make Eden happy.
She placed her hand on his soft cheek and tried to flatten out his hair.
'I love you too, ' she whispered back. Their lips touched gently. She closed her eyes as he pressed his against hers. All of the bad energy that had made its way into their

day evaporated as they became one again. She cupped his face with her hands. They had never gotten so lost in a kiss before, this one was magical, it had depth to it. His kiss wasn't like the ones you see in the movies, where they kiss and make up in the rain under the bright moon. No, it was the promise for a forever, for passion, for realness in a world where nothing has a happy ending. He promised her, that night, a happy ending. To her, this was the best thing someone could ever promise.

Juliet sat Eden up and looked at her dead in the eye. 'Don't you have to meet someone this morning?' She asked as she tried to flatten down Eden's wet hair.
'Um… yeah, I should probably go and get ready.' Eden stood up, fixing the towel that was wrapped around her body. Juliet passed her the clothes that now lay sprawled across the floor. The album was also on the floor. They both stared at it.
'I'll keep hold of this,' Juliet finally said as she leant down to pick it up.
'Just don't throw it away, please,' Eden pleaded. Juliet nodded and went to her room, shutting the door behind her.
Eden got changed, slowly, but at least she did it. Her mind was racing, she knew she had to talk to Archie, she had to. It would give her closure to the past which she had been holding on to for so long now. It would enable her to accept that it really was all over.
Sometimes, people say things that they never really mean. It happens quite often when you're in love. Young

and in love specifically. You haven't understood the world properly, you're too wrapped up in the moment to realise you said the most stupid thing a person could ever say. You can never promise someone a happy ending, because in life, happy endings don't always come true. Archie promised Eden a happy ending. And Eden thought that her happy ending was with him. Obviously, he was too in love to realise that together they couldn't write the perfect happy ending. Do perfect happy endings even exist now?

Eight

It was a terrible thing to admit, but sometimes Eden liked turning up late because she felt like it was showing she really wanted to be there, and so made every effort to do so. She could see Loren standing out in the rain, the wind blowing through her hair making it look like a horse's tail. She wanted to run so that Loren wasn't waiting, but felt that would seem a little too excited. She wanted this to be over and done with, so she could get back to everything else. Eden gulped as she neared her, smiling at anyone who passed her because it seemed like the nicest thing to do.
'Hey, sorry I'm late, I left my phone and had to run back to get it,' Eden lied as she greeted Loren and opened the door to the cafe for her.
'It's okay, I like to just stand and take in my surroundings sometimes. Clears my mind and all,' Loren explained and found a table by the window for the two of them to sit at. They sat down and smiled at each other. Eden had never been to this cafe before. It had a vintage, rustic vibe to it, with naked brick on the walls and rustic wooden flooring. The lights were a dark shade of yellow and gave off a

golden glow. The room was therefore darker than usual, it was nicer to the eye, Eden thought. She could smell the raw scent of coffee beans being ground just paces away from where she was sitting.

'It's a nice little place,' Loren smiled and said, 'I come here quite often, to write mainly. It's quiet so I can concentrate.'

They ordered their drinks at the counter and sat back down again.

'So, where are you from?' Loren asked. She was stirring her coffee gently.

'Iowa originally, I moved here, um, September, with my friend.' She stumbled a bit, factually she had moved here in September, but not with Juliet.

'So literally the middle of nowhere huh, you know I've never been to any of those types of states. I've always been a city girl,' Loren replied. Her confidence amazed Eden despite meeting her through a support group.

'You're from New York then?'

'Born and bred, couldn't think of anywhere else I'd rather live if I'm being honest.' Loren rolled up the sleeves of her sweatshirt she was wearing. Eden wasn't sure whether to be shocked, or sorry for what she saw. Loren clearly wasn't hiding them anymore. There were scars, lots of them, marked all the way up her arms to her elbows. She studied them, but so that Loren couldn't tell she was looking. Eden had never seen scars before. She didn't know how to react, how to talk. She just sat there. How could someone hate themself so much that they cut themself, she thought. Loren noticed her looking and sat up straight in her chair.

'When I was fourteen I started to starve myself. I wanted to look like everyone else, skinny and perfect. It got to a point where I almost died, and these,' she placed her arms flat on the table so that Eden could see properly, 'this was my way of letting out the pain.'
One wrong word and Eden could deeply offend Loren. She had heard of people who harmed themselves, but had never seen it before. Her eyes wandered over her arms for a few seconds before looking back up at Loren.
'But you're okay now?' Was all she could ask.
'Getting better, it's something I'll never get over. Things like this aren't just a phase you see, they stick with you for life. I've just learnt how to deal with it.'
Eden liked the way Loren acted. She didn't put on a show when she spoke, she felt from the heart. Her words were raw and real, in a way, Eden could relate to Loren, and in some ways she couldn't. Eden had never cut herself before, but she had starved herself. She had never been to a mental health hospital, but she had tried to take her own life. There were aspects of their lives that intertwined with each other. Similar but not the same.
The cafe emptied and filled up again. People were coming in to shelter themselves from the heavy rain that continued to fall over the city. Why did people leave their homes knowing that rain was a common occurrence in New York? Eden felt that she had to return any of the questions Loren asked her, it was only fair. She was more talkative than Juliet, she realised. Why Eden befriended talkative people she did not know?

'Are you in college? You seem so bright not to be,' Eden asked as another drink arrived for the both of them.
'Creative Writing at Columbia University,' Loren said proudly. Eden wasn't expecting that.
'Oh My God, that's amazing, I... I didn't realise. Why aren't you there now?' She brought her drink up to her mouth as she finished speaking.
'I don't have classes in the morning today, but I'll have to leave soon, they're pretty strict over there,' Loren explained.
'No wonder, that's like, one of the best places to go. So you're pretty serious about becoming a writer then?' Eden had now swapped to being the question master. They were flooding out of her like a dormant volcano erupting, once in a blue moon.
'That's the goal. I want to share my work with everyone.' Loren nodded. She had on these huge round glasses, a bit like Harry Potter, that made her look like a total dork, but it suited her. The few pieces that hadn't made it into her ponytail shaped her small sunken face and covered up her hollow cheekbones. She was happy though. That's what really mattered.
The music playing in the background switched, Eden knew the song. Of course she did, he was everywhere. Archer King, teenage superstar. To Eden, Archie.
'Oh I love this song,' Loren tapped her fingers on the table to the slow rhythm of the music. All of his songs were slow, that was his style. Eden tried to make out a smile as she tried to agree with Loren. Obviously she liked the

song, it was for her, but now she liked it for different reasons.

There he was, standing on the edge of the car park, his hands outstretched in front of him. Eden's mum saw him first. She tapped Eden on the shoulder and pointed to where Archie was standing. Her face when she turned around and saw him beamed with delight and excitement and all the happy feelings you could ever feel all at once. He wore a matted black leather jacket with a plaid shirt underneath and washed out black jeans that now looked a shade of grey if anything. He was different, his new 'style change' as Eden sometimes called it made him look more confident. He was becoming a true rock god.

Eden ran up to him and flung her arms around his neck. He picked her up and swung her around before pressing his lips against hers as she was still just above ground in his arms. Not seeing each other in two weeks had been the longest they had been apart. Two weeks was too long to not hold each other and look into each other's eyes, and just be in the moment.

'I missed you,' he said as she let Eden down and stroked her hair which she let down today. Special days called for special hairstyles.

'I missed you too,' she replied and let Archie kiss her forehead before picking up his suitcase and guitar and walking towards her mum. He waved at her, and she waved back, leaning against the side of her car, which needed replacing soon. The shell of it was dented in places and the colour was fading quickly.

'Thanks for the ride Mrs Harper,' he smiled at her mum and placed his belongings in the back before climbing in with Eden next to him.
'No problem, Eden told me your parents were out of town. Couldn't miss out on picking up a soon to be world famous rock star,' she laughed. Eden rolled her eyes and leant over so that her head lay perfectly on his shoulder.
'So how was it out there?' Mrs Harper asked after they had set out on the road back home. The airport was close enough for them to not fall asleep on the journey home.
'Yeah it was great, got introduced to the label, met a few people who said they were excited to see where I was heading, which was promising,' he started.
'Did you record anything?' Eden wondered. She was playing with a loose piece of hair that hung from his face. Its curl wrapped perfectly around her finger.
'You'll have to wait and see.' He tapped her nose and she giggled. Although they couldn't see it, Mrs Harper smiled indefinitely. As long as they were happy, she was happy. It was all she ever wanted in Eden's life. Outside the window Eden could see endless rows of fields and ranches. They were coloured yellow and green and you could smell the freshness of the air around them. But all she wanted to do was look at Archie, it's all she ever wanted to do.
By the time they arrived back the grey clouds had elapsed into a darker night. Archie's house was empty, his parents were out. They pulled up outside just before seven, her mum turned around, but they were fast asleep. She had never seen two people fall asleep so beautifully.

Eden decided to stay with Archie for the rest of the evening. She waved goodbye to her mum, who by now had become used to Eden spending her evenings with Archie. To Eden, home was with Archie.

His house was small, but tidy. It never had a spot of untidiness anywhere, his parents always made sure to keep it spotless for guests. The curtains were drawn closed tightly as she looked around. Archie bent down as his dog jumped up on him and covered him in wet sloppy kisses. It knocked him over and he let it walk all over him, his muddy paws making brown prints on his top. Eden wiped them off with her fingers and smiled.

'When will your parents be back?' Eden asked as they placed his things down at the bottom of the staircase. He wrapped his arms around her waist as he walked up behind her.

'Tomorrow,' he whispered into her ear, 'which gives me time to show you something.'

He pulled out a CD from his bag and placed it into the player next to the TV. She followed him and sat down on the sofa. The disk started to play a song she hadn't heard before. A new one. He had written it whilst he was away maybe. There was something about it that seemed different. Maybe it was because he had written and recorded it in a professional studio. Maybe it was that she hadn't heard his voice sing in weeks and she had been yearning for it for so long. Whatever it was, Eden let her mind be tangled in the music she was hearing. To Eden, there were songs that she heard and liked, or there were songs she heard and felt that they had been a part of her for so long, she just didn't know it. This song was exactly that. Something inside of her awakened as she listened to it, a fire ignited.

Archie placed his hand on top of hers as the song came to a close. He noticed a tear emerge from the corner of her eye, which he softly wiped away with his finger. She didn't look up at him. Her face was paler than usual and glistened with the water that slowly fell from her eyes. She had tucked her hair behind her ears which showed her impressively defined cheekbones. Archie cupped her face in his hands and moved it so she was looking up to him. He rubbed his thumb across her cheek and chin, staring deeply into her eyes. Eden always felt that the most love you can give is through the eyes because they hold the most emotion and the most sorrow. The most pain and the most adoration. Her eyes told the most romantic story he had ever read.

'*I can't lose you.* I wrote it on the plane whilst travelling out to New York. Whatever happens now, you stay by my side, forever.' He brought her in and hugged her tightly. She paused and let him wrap himself around her, before she did the same to him. The fifth song.

Eden looked up at Loren, who was still humming softly to the song still after it had finished.

'You know apparently the person he wrote this whole album for, he broke up with her just before it was released,' Loren announced. They had been silent for sometime whilst listening to the song. Eden acknowledged her statement, but didn't say anything. How could she?

'I wonder who it was for? The album expresses so much love and emotion towards this person, it's a shame that it basically means nothing now,' Loren continued to say.
The problem was, it did still mean something. Just because it was over, didn't mean the feelings had suddenly vanished.
Eden wanted to go home. She had a sudden urge to want to cry on top of her bed for the rest of the day. Seeing Loren was nice, she liked meeting up with someone who was similar in some ways. But she couldn't handle it today.
'It was so nice meeting with you today,' Eden finally said as she started to put on her coat she had left on the back of her chair. Loren looked up, shocked, and then smiled. She processed what Eden had said, she thought it had ended too soon, or maybe she said something that offended her.
'Yes, yes thank you,' she replied and copied Eden by getting up and tucking her chair neatly under the table, 'we should do this again.'
Loren walked around the table and gave Eden a hug. Eden could smell her strong Upper East Side perfume as she embraced her. They walked out of the cafe and said goodbye to each other again before going their separate ways.
Her love for Archie would never die, she realised. She would always love him, and maybe, in some alternate universe, they were still together. Because Eden believed in cosmic love. A love that is so full of emotion and power, and has so much significance, that it becomes amazingly

unique. There was nothing that could compare to the love Archie and Eden had for each other. In her mind, even before the world started and the universe was created, their love had been preassigned. They were fated. By the stars. They had been chosen to be together, and you can't go against the laws of the universe, can you? So, she believed that he would come back to her, one day.

When Juliet returned home she found Eden lying fast asleep on her bed, hugging the album she thought she had hidden so carefully in her room. Nothing is ever hidden from Eden.

Nine

Eden didn't know what was coming to her when she sat down at the table the following morning. Juliet nudged the most recent newspaper towards her and looked down into her cup of coffee. Her eyes read and reread what was on the front page. She wanted to make sure she wasn't seeing things. She wanted to make sure she wasn't still sleeping. Eden pinched herself, slapped her thigh, and then left the room and lay back down on her bed, before screaming into her pillow. Almost loud enough so that the neighbouring apartments could hear her.
She knew this day would come soon enough. Some people just move on easily and are able to put everything behind them. She just never thought Archie would be that person.
Eden lay there a little longer before returning back into the kitchen, where she found Juliet, slouched over, and reading the newspaper. She sat back down and Juliet pushed the newspaper back over to her. Eden read it again. And again. And then again. She traced her fingers over the picture that had been printed. The black ink

stained the tips of her fingers and smudged the image slightly.

'Do you want to talk about it?' Juliet asked. She had given it time before she even said something. One wrong word and they could go back to square one Eden downing pills and crying herself to sleep.

'I think it's best not to.' Eden shrugged and turned the page. She had read it so much she couldn't bare to even look at that front page anymore. Her mind found it hard to picture what she had just read. But it was true. Every single word of it. He had moved on. There was now a new person to write songs about. She was the first. And now there was a second.

Shore's was unusually busy later that day when Eden had arrived. Before she even walked into the store she could see a crowd of people inside. Some browsing, some talking. The old busted sign that originally stood over the store had been replaced by a freshly painted one. The place was more put together. Eden didn't like it. She preferred the rustic, old place that it normally was. Her eyes peered through the window before she opened the door and heard the bell ring. Mr Shore waved at her from behind the counter. She smiled vaguely back and made her way through the strangely large crowd of people that had gathered in the store.

'Why's it so busy today?' She asked, placing her bag under the counter and sitting down on the brown stool behind her.

'New stock. We got loads of that Archer King album you took home the other day, plus lots of other stuff. But the people are really here for King.' Mr Shore pointed at the shelf which had an almost glistening shine to it of new records. He was smiling excitedly like a new puppy when it got a new toy.

'He really is everywhere,' she muttered.

'Apparently everyone's buying them because he's in town for a concert. Sold out Madison Square Garden two nights in a row,' he added. Eden nodded, like she was surprised. She remembered him telling her, before it all happened, that he had sold out Madison Square Garden. He had been so excited to finally perform in his dream location.

'Are you going?' He wondered as another person walked into the shop. They were coming and going like flies. She had blanked out, not on purpose, but she didn't want to hear anymore of Archer King that day.

'No.' She smiled and picked up a box of records that had been collecting dust under the counter. Archer King was everywhere. He was everywhere in other people's lives, yet he had made himself scarce in hers.

After they had sold the vast majority of his albums people started to empty out of the shop, and eventually so did Mr Shore, leaving Eden to lock up after she shut shop. It was mid afternoon, no one really came in after three. She finished clearing the counter of receipts and loose cash, and then pulled out the stool under the piano. This would be interesting.

Her fingers brushed lightly against the keys of the piano. She didn't press down, not yet at least. The instrument stood upright against the back wall. It had collected dust over the years it had been there, which had been a long

time. It was brown, faded to be exact, and the keys had gone a slightly off white colour like when white trainers finally become wearable after them being pristine for so long. She looked behind her. Nothing. The piano was almost yearning for her to play it. It was calling her from within.
Eden pressed down on the keys and closed her eyes. She let her fingers do their work, playing one note after the next. Making music. It was like Eden had entered a trance created by the sweet music that was coming from the instrument. She was being lifted by the music that she hadn't played in months, and she liked it. Eden couldn't tell how long she played for, she didn't keep track of the time, just what she was playing. She could feel herself being lifted up by the music and into the sky, the stars shined like a thousand bright lights beaming at her. Eden wanted to reach out and touch all of them, hold them tightly in her hands. She had always been fascinated with the stars and what they were. Maybe because she felt everything was drawn in the stars. Because stars hold destinies, and Eden believed in destiny.
There was a clap from behind her. Eden jumped and turned around. He looked exactly like Archie, but it wasn't. The same messy dark hair on his head, the same hypnotising eyes, and the same black clothing. He smiled in the same way too, like he was looking at his whole world. He stopped clapping after some time, but still continued to smile in a slightly freakish way.
'That was... amazing,' he said as Eden stood up from the piano stool and walked around him to the counter.

'Thank you.' She looked down and replied shyly. His boots were sleek and black and had metal studs on the heel. He looked like some sort of biker dude that was supposed to be part of a gang.
'How long have you been playing?' He asked and followed her to the counter.
'All my life.' Her answers were short and simple.
'I'm Ezra.' He held out his hand for Eden to shake. She glanced over his shoulder, and then took his hand, staring at his whole black attire and freakishly handsome eyes.
'Eden,' she replied. He looked around the shop before turning to face her again, who was slightly nervous as to where he was leading her.
'I actually came in here to get a present for my mother. You don't happen to have any Rumours albums? Fleetwood Mac,' he added. She nodded and led him to where they had one stored. Eden reached up and pulled it out off the shelf and brushed the dust off before handing it to him. He was a family man clearly. You don't just give a Rumours album to someone for it to mean nothing.
'What's your favourite song on the album?' She asked as she carefully packaged it up in the old newspapers on the desk. He thought for a minute, Eden noticed how his forehead creased as he thought of an answer. She always found it sweet when boys did that.
'I think everyone wants you to think *Dreams* is the best, when actually I think *Songbird* is. I mean, it's sung to someone who they consider the love of their life. She wishes him no pain, she believes the sun only shines for

him. Imagine having a song written about you like that,' he started to explain. But he didn't stop there.

'When she's by his side, when they're together she feels at peace. They've been through everything together, she wishes him everything... happiness. Their love was written in the stars, it was meant to happen. She has never loved someone this much before.'

That hit Eden in places she didn't know she could be hit. Of course he didn't know her pains and her troubles that she had experienced.

'I agree,' she said quietly. Truthfully, she did agree. That song had made its way into her heart and made its home there. She and Archie always used to listen to it.

'Really? I think it's such an underrated song, that people just look over. It's gut-wrenchingly sad, that she wishes him everything, because they are no longer together. She loves him, but he doesn't love her back. A bittersweet story of letting go of your loved one.' Ezra pulled up a stool by him and sat down in front of Eden, clenching the now nicely packaged album in his fists.

'I think it's a final goodbye song. It's a very sad, very loving, very kind goodbye song,' she spoke and gave a weak smile. If only Archie had given her a song like that. But he hadn't. Instead, he left her nothing. Just an album to rub into her face he had been more successful than her.

Eden always feared that her and Archie's love story would follow the lines of that song. She knew what it meant, and yet she still listened to it. If anything, it was karma for listening to it on repeat. Because her story turned out

exactly like how it was described. She loves him too much, and he doesn't feel the same way. She wishes him all the happiness that she felt when she was around him.
'What other artists do you like?' He tried to change the subject. Talking about heartbreak clearly didn't make Eden happy he realised.
'Old school music. Bowie, ABBA, The Beatles, Queen. The classics really.'
'So you like your British music huh?' He joked sarcastically.
'I suppose I do.' She finally gave a fully fledged smile, and laughed a little.
Ezra was so similar to Archie, in so many ways, and yet he was so different. It was like they had been separated at birth and raised on two different planets. His laughter and happiness managed to absorb itself into Eden. There wasn't a moment then that she didn't feel like she wanted to jump off a cliff, or down a bottle of pills. For the first that month she could feel pure happiness inside of her. Fluttering around and digging itself in so that it was engraved in her body.
'I should probably get going, my mums gonna wonder where I am soon,' he said, looking over his shoulder at the street outside, and then smiling at Eden. He kicked the stool away and thread his arms through the jacket he had worn.
'It was really nice meeting you.' She weaved her fingers in and out of each other.
'Same, I'm glad I met you,' he replied. He picked up his purchase and made his way to the door. Even his walk

made her happy. 'Oh, you should come to my mum's birthday party. I don't have anyone to bring with me, I think she'd really like you.'

'But I've only just met you, I don't even know your mum,' she responded. He opened the door slightly, just enough so that the bell didn't ring. It was now dark outside, and the rain still fell.

'Yeah, but I've got a good feeling about you. I'll call you,' he clicked his fingers and pointed, before leaving the store and walking away. She watched him go, before turning around and sitting back at the chair she had got up from. Shit. *I've got a good feeling about you.* What was that supposed to mean? She couldn't start something new. She didn't think she was able to start something new. But they had related to each other in so many ways, it seemed silly not to. He was utterly, most certainly, and definitely gorgeous and handsome in so many ways. But that didn't mean that it was the right time. Archie had moved on. Why couldn't she? Surely she was able to go and be with someone else. It wasn't like it was a crime or anything. Maybe that's how she let go. She didn't need to go to Archie and confess that she was finally moving on. He didn't even know that she had been trying to cling on for dear life. Quite literally.

And Ezra was sweet. He made his move and he did it well. Effortlessly if anything. But he looked so much like Archie. It would be like she wasn't even trying to find someone different. Because he was a walking talking Archer King who just so happened not to be him.

Ezra didn't even try to wait for Eden to text him first. As soon as she had shut up shop for that day and had started walking home she felt a buzz in her pocket. Eden pulled out her phone, and despite the rain heavily pouring down on it making the screen wet, she didn't put it away.
6pm. This Friday. 456 W 25th St. Hope you'll come - Ezra.
Eden didn't need to think twice before answering.
Thanks for the invite. I can't wait. Any dress code needed?
He replied immediately.
Haha, no. Turn up in a Santa outfit for all I care.
Eden laughed as she looked down at her phone whilst walking.
Watch me ;).
She had never felt this confident before. Not with Juliet. And not even with Loren. Ezra had in some ways, given her a second chance at everything. He had opened a door that Eden didn't know existed before.
Please don't actually turn up as Santa. Wait until Christmas for that.
She dodged a skater who was coming her way.
Damn it, you got my hopes up.
Eden got home and opened the door. She was greeted with a not so nice surprise.
'Oh my god at least go into your room,' she exclaimed.
Juliet was lying on the sofa in front of her. Jason was on top. Their legs were intertwined and she was pretty sure Jason was half naked, but she didn't even want to check. She shut the door and pressed her back against it,

hearing the other two move until everything was silent again. When she walked in she threw herself onto the bed and held her phone above her head, scanning her eager eyes over the message she had just received.

I was being serious earlier. I really liked meeting you. There's something we both have. She read, smiling as she processed every last letter.

Like our affinity for Fleetwood Mac? She texted back and held her phone close to her chest. It buzzed.

And that. Fleetwood Mac is superior.

They really were superior.

I want to be hearing that album you just bought on Friday night. Otherwise I'll never speak to you again. It was the first time she had sent a sarcastic, funny, message to someone in a long time.

Aye aye captain.

For the entire evening the two of them exchanged messages. Her smile didn't drop from her face. Everytime a new message arrived her heart grew two sizes. There was something about Ezra that made her want to start anew. No one was pushing her this time, it was all her. He didn't push her into talking about her past, he just wanted to experience the moment then, over the phone. Just by a few texts.

As Eden got into bed for real, at just gone ten, he called her, and she answered.

'What's your favourite colour?' he asked as they got into their conversation.

'Why are you asking me about my favourite colour?' She laughed and rested her head on her pillow, looking up at the tall ceiling.

'Because you can find out a lot about someone from their favourite colour. You see my favourite colour is black, I wear a lot of black, I'm independent, just like the colour, because it's so different and doesn't care about standing out and making a statement,' He explained. He could hear her giggle on the other side of the phone. That made him smile.

'Black isn't a colour. Everyone knows that,' she stated. Scientifically, she was right. Black was the absence of all colours. When there is no light, everything is black. You cannot see colour when all there is is blackness. Therefore, black isn't a colour.

'Black is totally a colour. What did you learn in school? That red is an animal?' He replied sarcastically.

'No I was taught that black is the absence of all colours. When everything is dark, there is no colour, it's only black. You cannot see a colour through another colour, therefore, black is not a colour.' Eden was somewhat proud of using her minimal amount of knowledge to explain to Ezra that he was wrong.

'Stop being such a know it all,' he muttered, and they both laughed.

'Just because I know that, doesn't make me smart in any way,' she added.

'So come on then, what's your favourite colour?' He asked again. His voice was smooth and relaxing, it made her want to fall asleep there and then.

'Technically, you haven't answered yet, so I could ask you the same question,' she said proudly. Eden wiped away the hair that had fallen over the face.

'You're being sneaky,' he replied, 'I'll get back to you on that one,' he added.

'Then I guess you'll have to wait to hear about my favourite colour,' she answered.

'I'll wait.'

He would wait for her. He would do that?

'Well, I'm off to sleep now,' she said in an attempt to end the call, although she didn't want to. She could talk to Ezra forever and not get bored.

'I'll see you in dreamland.' And he ended the call.

Archie used to say that. Archie would say that at the end of every phone call. He would see her in dreamland. And he did. Her dreams of him were like magic, they were real. Eden didn't believe that she could see anyone else in dreamland. Dreamland was only made for her and Archie.

'In dreamland we'll meet,' she muttered and looked up at the ceiling, although she wished it was the stars. She'd look at the stars any time.

Ten

There was faint out of tune whistling coming from the kitchen the following morning. Eden couldn't bare to hear it any longer. She threw on the closest jumper she had and walked to the kitchen. Obviously she had a feeling who it was.
'Morning,' Jason said and looked over his shoulder. He was wearing the bare minimum. The hob was on and he was frying up bacon, which sizzled and crackled. Juliet never made Eden cooked breakfasts, like ever.
'Hey,' she waved at him then sat down at the table. There was a newspaper, she flinched before deciding to read it. Archer could be in it, he could not be in it.
That morning Eden learnt that Jason had stayed the night, with Juliet, and that they were now officially a couple. She could see that one coming from a mile off. Eden liked Jason, he was sensible, and he took care of Juliet. That made one of them.
Jason was one of those people who everybody liked, he just gave off that vibe. He was kind, so people were kind

to him. Eden was glad that Juliet had met him, but she worried. She didn't want her to fall in love quickly, like she did, and then have her heart shattered into a million pieces. Eden didn't want her to end up like she did. Broken.

'You want some?' Jason pointed at the bacon in the saucepan.

'Yeah sure, thanks,' she smiled and replied.

'Have you had any good records at the shop lately?' Eden could tell he was trying to make conversation. If she could hear correctly, there were wedding bells in the distance, and she would be maid of honour, so she had to be friends with Jason.

'Every record is interesting, we got some Aretha Franklin, Michael Jackon, and Louis Armstrong the other day,' Eden explained. He plated up some of the bacon and Eden sliced up the fresh bread that was on the table. They never had fresh bread, today was clearly special.

'I love Louis Armstrong, my dad always played jazz music back at home, so I've just grown up loving it.' Jason gave her the plate and passed the ketchup over.

'Jazz music always makes me feel at home, although I grew up in Iowa which is the complete opposite to New Orleans and the southern states,' she laughed.

'Iowa is a pretty desolate state, no offence, ' he added. They both smiled and laughed.

'None taken, nothing goes on there. I think the only reason Juliet didn't do English at Iowa University was because she wanted to leave the state.' Eden started eating her bacon sandwich he had made her. There was a jug of orange juice on the table as well, which she poured into her cup.

'Where's Juliet?' She asked.

'In the shower I think,' he replied and pointed to the closed bathroom door. It was closed, just like the time she had closed it before she collapsed onto the floor and almost died. Eden smiled at Jason and continued eating.

When Juliet arrived Eden felt awkward and out of place, so she left. She wasn't jealous or anything, she just didn't want to watch the excessive affection being exchanged between the two new love birds.

Jason left soon after, half dressed to Eden, but he left. Juliet had this flushed sort of look as he kissed her and walked out of the door. She had her dark curly hair tied up in what looked like a bun, and her dark was freshly washed so it gave off a glowing light. She was pretty, wrapped up in her dressing gown and wearing her blue slippers which Eden had bought her for her birthday last July. She didn't even need to wear slippers in July.

'I've got the day completely free, if you wanted to do something. It seems like ages since we've actually spent some time together,' Juliet said and sat down on Eden's bed next to her. She crossed her legs and brought the duvet over her knees, smiling into Eden's eyes.

'Yeah,' she answered, 'I'd love that.'

'So, tell me about this guy I heard you speaking to last night. Is he cute?' Juliet asked.

'The cutest, but I'm taking it slow. Not sure if he is, but I'm interested to see where it goes,' she explained. Truthfully he was cute, that wasn't a lie.

'Are you ready for a relationship, you've only ever been in one... and that didn't end... well,' Juliet hesitated as she spoke. This could highly offend Eden or not bother her at all.

'I think I am, yeah,' she lied. She wasn't ready. She wasn't over Archie. She still loved Archie, she could never love anyone else like Archie. But no one could know that. Not even Juliet.

'Well, I'm happy for you, I'm proud of you.' Juliet grabbed Eden's wrist and smiled gleefully. Why did Juliet always say that? Maybe it was just a way of telling Eden that she would always be there for her. The one thing Eden had to hold onto now was Juliet, she couldn't let her slip away too.

'We could do a major movie marathon, the weather's awful for the whole day, and I don't want to have a second shower,' Juliet joked. Eden nodded and almost pushed Juliet off the bed as she got out and pulled out clothes to wear for the day. Comfy clothes obviously. There would be no jeans in sight today.

'So what happened to you applying for NYU music?' Juliet asked as she walked back in, dressed and looking like the human version of a soft pillow.

'I don't want to go, I can find my way without a degree. Besides, I like my job at the record shop,' she added. They had made some sort of fort around the sofa and the TV so that they could hibernate there for the day.

'You can't work at that shop for the rest of your life,' Juliet said.

'I know, but until I get back on my feet with music, I think it's fine.'

The 'fort' as it appeared to be, was used with both Eden and Juliet's bedding. Eden was a little creeped out at the fact that they were the sheets Juliet had had on her bed when she had sex with Jason, but she decided to put that past her and focus on other things.

'Okay well take it out of the covers then, we'll just have the inside stuff,' Eden gave in. Juliet pulled out the duvet from inside the sheet and placed it on the floor so that it looked like they were sitting on a blanket of snow.

Since the age of sixteen the two of them had made a list of all the films they wanted to watch together, some of them were films they'd seen before, some of them not.

'We could binge all the Harry Potter's?' Juliet suggested as she climbed in under the fort and pulled the blanket up over her knees.

'I think I've watched them too many times,' Eden confessed. 'Titanic?'

'I don't think I've ever watched Titanic in my eighteen years of existence.' Juliet tried searching for it on the TV.

'Then you've missed out my friend.' Eden pressed play on the film and they cwtched up together under the blankets. It reminded her of the times they used to have when they were younger, more impressionable, and much freer. She enjoyed the film, she wasn't sure if Juliet did.

'I don't understand, Jack could have fit on that door. Why did he stay in the water?' Juliet asked as the film entered the credits.

'Don't ask me, that scene has been talked about for years.'

'Did you cry?' Juliet looked at Eden's face, 'you did cry, why am I not surprised?'

Of course Eden cried. How could she not? She didn't want to see herself in Rose, and Archie in Jack, but she did. And how it came to an end all too quickly. She realised she wasn't crying at the film, she had seen it too many times, she just got used to the emotion. She was crying at herself. And the pain had come back again. It wasn't going away.

'I can see why you like that film so much,' Juliet said as she tried to wipe away the tears that were falling from Eden's face.

'You can?'

'Yeah, tragic love story, that's your genre.'

Eden sat up from where she had been slouching against the sofa. Her face wanted to scowl, but she didn't. But what Juliet had just said, haunted her, if anything.

'Tragic love story? That's my genre? Just because I've had a tragic love story doesn't mean it's the only language I speak now,' Eden spoke, there was a small sense of anger in her voice.

'Well... no, but you know,' Juliet started, before she was interrupted.

'No I don't know. And you don't know how I feel, you never have. You know this is the first time in weeks we've actually spent some proper time together, and it's all because of that stupid Jason.' Eden threw the blanket off of her and crawled out of the now half broken 'fort' they had made. Juliet followed unwillingly.

'So you think I don't deserve to be happy? To finally find someone who understands me, because you sure as hell don't,' Juliet's voice got louder and more intense. 'It's called growing up and being an adult. Maybe you should try it, you'd learn a lot more than just clinging onto the past. Archie isn't coming back. Move on.'

Eden's eyes grew fierce. Juliet was right, no matter how hard Eden looked at it. But that didn't stop her.

'Get out,' she demanded.

'You can't kick me out of my own house,' Juliet replied, She crossed her arms and stood firmly in front of Eden.

'Get the hell out,' Eden yelled.

Juliet rolled her eyes, swung her handbag over her shoulder and picked up her jacket. The door slammed shut and Eden stood there in the middle, silent. The room was eerie and quiet, the echoes of the door were still somehow circling the ceiling. She fell slowly to the ground, her knees hitting the floor and making a painful sound. She let her hair fall loosely below her shoulders and wiped away with her sleeve, a tear from her eye. But it wasn't long before more tears emerged from the corners of her eyes. Without instinct she pulled the sheets and duvet covers, pulling all the contents of the coffee table with it. Magazines were spread randomly across the room. She flung the cushions behind her and picked up the lamp. It had a brown body and a gorgeous baby blue lamp shade. Smashed. She threw it on the ground in front of her. The books on the bookcase, Juliet's books, she scattered across the floor. Some ripped, but she didn't care. She had ripped apart the entire room.There were pictures of her and Juliet hung up on the wall. They were soon shattered on the floor and the pictures ripped and fell to the floor like snowflakes.

Eden stepped back and looked at everything. It was a mess. She had always seen these scenes in movies where people have a complete breakdown and destroyed everything. Well, she had just done that. Eden fell against the side of her bed and bawled. Her face was hot and red and she felt ill. But she wasn't sure what from. Eden grabbed her phone that was sitting on her bed and texted Ezra.

Can you come over? Now?

She wasn't expecting a reply though, they met yesterday. He had probably forgotten about her. She got a reply five minutes later.

I'll be there ASAP

Eden sent him her address, and then looked up at the room. She could try and tidy it, but it wouldn't make a difference. She was still messy on the inside.

Ezra arrived ten minutes later. He knocked on the door and she opened it, still red and blotted and completely messed up.

'What's wrong?' He asked as he saw her face and was let in.

'Don't talk.' She pressed her finger on his lips, closed the door behind him and then pinned him to the wall and mounted her lips on his. He didn't hesitate. She wrapped her arms around his neck, and his around hers. There

was no love though. They didn't stop kissing, she didn't want to. Her mind was taken off of Juliet, the destruction she had just made to their apartment, even Archie for a minute. His hair was wet from the rain he had just walked through as she ran her fingers through it, just like she did with Archie. It felt like Archie.
His skin was smooth against hers. His everything was smooth against hers. All of her imperfections somehow were smoothed out by him. But that didn't make her stop thinking about Archie. Every kiss she made she felt she was betraying him.
Why didn't Ezra pull away? Was he enjoying it?
She felt so secure around Ezra, but that didn't mean she was instantly over Archie. For starters, they looked the same. That wasn't exactly called getting over your ex. Eden thought that meeting Ezra and being with him would make her get over Archie, but it didn't. In fact, it did the exact opposite. She only wanted Archie more. Juliet was right, she was always right.
'Why did you ask me to come over?' Ezra asked as Eden rested her head on his chest and danced her fingers across his stomach.
'No particular reason,' she replied. Eden lifted her head and leant on her elbow, looking deeply into his eyes. She thought she was looking into Archie's eyes for a minute.
'And what happened here? Is it usually like this?' Ezra did the same and leant on his elbow. Eden looked behind her at the room. It was still messy, and yet it still wasn't finished.

'My roommate and I were just cleaning things out,' she sighed.
'By smashing lamps and picture frames?'
'We never liked that lamp anyway.'
'Right.' He tucked her blonde hair behind her ears and cupped her face in his hand. Archie used to do the same. She thought she was looking at Archie.
He was everywhere, and yet he was nowhere. Archie was like this walking ghost that haunted Eden, he had wrapped himself inside her mind, and she couldn't forget him.

Eleven

It was wrong. She knew it was wrong, but all she wanted was Archie, and if Ezra was the closest she could get then so be it. Eden was living her past all over again, but with Ezra.

'I should probably start heading home,' Ezra said as he pulled on his sweatshirt over his head and slipped on the pair of converse he had arrived in. It was late morning, the kitchen smelt of freshly cooked pancakes, which Eden loved. The rain still fell though, would it ever stop?

'You could stay,' she replied as she finished the last drop of orange juice in her glass. He smiled at her and swung on his coat.

'I've got to go see my mum, but I'll call you.' He walked over to Eden and gave her a kiss. She was taken back slightly, but didn't stop him. She didn't realise they were in that sort of relationship yet. His breath tasted like warm coffee. Sweet.

'Bye.' He closed the door behind him and left Eden sitting there, alone, again.

She looked around the apartment, it was still an absolute tip. She didn't know when, or if Juliet would be coming back soon, but she sure as hell didn't want her seeing the place like this. Eden started humming a tune under her breath as she picked up broken pieces of glass and torn pictures. But it wasn't the mess she focused on, it was the song. She didn't even realise what she was humming, until her eyes had welled up with tears and she was on the floor reminiscing about Archie.

He held her hand and pulled her through the trees, moving the branches out of the way as they walked. Some still managed to hit her face, lightly though. He had his guitar strung to his back, he almost never left the house without it now. They came into a clearing, one Eden had never been to before. How did Archie know all of these places? The sun had been in their favour that day, April had decided to not rain. She sat down on the grass and picked at it as he took out his guitar. His hair curled even more even more in the heat. Eden thought it was adorable. She thought he was adorable. That word made her gag usually, but using it for Archie gave it a whole new meaning.

'Why are we here?' She asked as he sat down in front of her and placed the guitar on his lap.

'I need help.' He pulled out a piece of paper from his pocket and placed it in front of them. It was the lyrics to a song. 'When I was playing it the other day something was missing.'

'What?' She took the lyrics and analysed them. They were adorable.

'You.'

She looked up sharply at him.

'You want me to sing this song?' She laughed.

'Yeah, as a duet. I thought we could sing it at the Spring Concert next week.' He smiled sweetly and looked up into her eyes. She had moved to kneel next to him.

'Well, let's hear it then.'

He strummed softly at the strings and started to sing. She followed the words on the paper in front of her and then looked up at him when it got to the chorus. He nodded and raised his eyebrows. Eden took a small breath and then joined in. Their voices mixed perfectly together like jelly and icecream. Even the birds somehow joined in with their song. Eden looked deeply into his eyes, they were full of passion, and love. He was doing what he loved. Archie's voice could be defined as perfect by Eden. She loved it, she loved him. The music echoed in the clearing. She rested her head on his shoulder as he sang, and she joined in on the chorus, barely, but it added something extra. It was the first time they had duetted one of Archie's songs. She had never been more in love with Archie then in that moment. She wanted to kiss him and touch him and sing with him for eternity.

He played the final chord and sang the final note. Eden placed both hands on his cheeks and kissed his forehead. Then his nose. Then his lips. She was the luckiest girl in the world, she thought. No man would write songs for her the way Archie did. She felt like he almost worshipped her in a way, but really it was the other way round. Eden couldn't comprehend how much she loved Archie. It was infinite.

'So, will you sing with me?' He asked calmly. The guitar had been placed to the side of him. Eden smiled, laughed and climbed onto his lap and kissed him. He was warm and welcomed her with open arms. He was adorable. Archie wrapped his arms around her and held her close to him. He didn't want to let go, she didn't want to let go. They walked back hand in hand to his car which was parked on the side of the road. The air was cool and there was a light breeze which made Eden's hair flow in the wind. Archie thought she looked like one of those surfer girls on the beach. He said she had beach hair, but they were nowhere near the beach.

'I've only ever been to the beach twice,' she replied as he ran his fingers through her waves.

'Well, why don't we go? To the beach. We could take a road trip down to Cali,' he added.

'When?'

'Next week?'

'My mum would never let me.' She swept one of his loose curls out of his face and ran her fingers down his cheek. He took hold of her hand and smiled.

'How about this summer? We'll plan it, I'll book us flights, and we can spend a week there. How does that sound?' He asked.

She smiled sweetly and sighed.

'It sounds wonderful.'

They drove back into town. The journey wasn't far, but Eden wanted it to last longer. She wanted to spend more time with Archie. All the time that ever existed, she wanted to spend it with him. The sky wasn't blue, it wasn't black, it was a misty shade of purple, like the colour of amethyst. She hummed gently to the song they had just sung. It was engraved in her brain. Cemented into her mind. It wasn't going.

'What's the song called?' She asked and looked up at him as he was driving.

'I... I don't know,' he answered, 'I guess i just hadn't thought of that.'

Eden sat up straight and stopped wrapping his curls around her fingers. They stopped at a red light. He turned to look at her.

'Do you have any ideas?' He asked, smiling deeply into her eyes.

She sat there and thought. She read and reread the lyrics he had given her, analysing each line, singing it in her head over and over again. She couldn't think of anything.

Eden brushed her hand over the record. His record. Her finger stopped at track number six. He had finally given it a name. It was nothing special. He hadn't put any thought into it. Clearly, he was just desperate to find another song to put on the album. To Archie this song meant the least, but to Eden it meant the world. *The Spring Concert Song* was the most unimaginative song title Eden could think of, and yet he named it that, because they sang it at the Spring Concert that year.

She pushed the record under her bed where she had left it and stood up. The place wasn't tidy, but it wasn't messy anymore. Eden walked over to the mirror hanging up on the wall. She was surprised she hadn't smashed it yesterday in her hour of rage. Her hair was greasy and disgusting and she had dark circles under her eyes and puffy red cheeks from where her tears had stained. She was a mess. She always had been.

Eden picked herself up, kind of, and went into the bathroom. She turned the shower on, it ran cold for a few seconds before steaming up the windows with its heat. A shiver was sent up her spine as she stepped over the side of the bath, carefully so as not to slip. The water ran through her blonde hair making the light colour of it turn a pasty shade of brown. She wanted the water to wash away her problems, that's what happens in the movies right? Instead she was only pushed deeper and darker into this well of loss. The cupboard next to her almost groaned for her, she could hear it calling her name. That's how she tried to end things last time. Only, it was just a pause button. She looked to the side of her, she could hardly see into the mirror, it was covered in hot steam from the shower. But to Eden, the shower wasn't hot. It turned from hot, to lukewarm, and then lukewarm to ice cold. And yet the steam was still there.

The water masked her tears. You couldn't tell if she was crying or not. But she was. Her fingers met her knotty hair, dancing into the mess it had made, ridding it of the knots time had given her. She caressed her skin with soap, she thought it would clean her of her troubles, but it only washed away the soft underbelly. Now you could see everything in broad daylight. The soap grazed her neck like his kisses, when he kissed her. More tears appeared from her eyes, or were they just drops of water from the shower head?

And then he was standing there with her, standing in front of her looking deeply into her eyes like he did before. He took a step towards her and wrapped his arms around her naked body and pressed his forehead against hers. He was soft. And then the water warmed up again. It dripped from his face and his eyelashes so that he could barely open his eyes. His lips were wet and begging for her to take them, so she did. She pressed her body against his even more and kissed him. She kissed him harder, like it was the only thing worth living for. He was the only thing to live for. Her fingers danced on the back of his neck as she wrapped his hair around them. Eden was smiling. His skin was like silk falling on hers, it wrapped around her and eased away all of her tensions. He was there with her. And then he wasn't.

Eden opened her eyes, the shower was still running onto her body. She looked around the bathroom, brushing the water out of her eyes. You could hear her breathing heavily like she had just won a race. But she hadn't. She'd lost. Eden climbed out of the shower and wrapped a towel around her body. She didn't turn the shower off. The bathroom door swung open and she ran out, looking around the apartment for Archie, but he wasn't there. She held tight to the towel surrounding her, that was the only thing keeping her together. Archie was nowhere. Her

breathing was louder and heavier and quicker. Her face was sweating, but she felt cold. Like ice had been thrown over her and she couldn't escape. She called out for him. There was no answer. Of course there was no answer. He hadn't been there. It was all in Eden's head.
When was Juliet coming back? Was she coming back? Would Eden ever see her again? Questions like these haunted her. The one time Eden needed Juliet the most, she was gone. She had scared her off with her crazy mind. Eden sat down in the kitchen, on the floor, and leaned against the cupboard. Her eyes were closed and she rested her head on the back. When she opened them a tear emerged from her eye. And this time, they really were tears.
She listened to *The Spring Concert Song* on repeat that day. Juliet didn't come back, she was gone, maybe forever. And so was Archie. She didn't eat, she didn't do anything. She skipped her shift down at Shore's Records, she lay on her bed all day listening to *The Spring Concert Song*. There wasn't even anything special about it, her voice had been faded into the background, just like she always was. She was fading still, if anything, faster than ever. People were fading her out of their lives, first Archie, now Juliet. Soon she'd just be fading out of life itself, and you can't turn back on that.
'Mum hi, I… I'm in trouble. I need your help, but I don't know what to do,' she said into the phone. 'No, no not with the police, I… I don't know what's happening. I could just really do with having you around.' She gulped as she spoke into the phone. 'No, I understand. Okay, forget I

called. Bye.' Eden threw the phone across the room. It landed on the sofa and then bounced off onto the carpet. Her knees came up to her chin and she wrapped her arms around them and buried her face into it. You could probably hear her crying from the other side of New York. If her mum couldn't help her, then who would?

The song was in her head, she hummed it as she started to pick up the rest of the broken picture frames and ripped photos. They were thrown into the black bin bag that lay on the sofa, but before she did, she looked through the broken halves of what were once whole. Pictures of her and Juliet back in Iowa, when they were younger, them at high school graduation. Happy memories. They could be printed out again if she came back. But she didn't, at least not that day. Eden stayed at home, alone, another day. And another. And another. She started to worry if Juliet had enough clothes, or if she had just bought new ones when she left. She didn't even know where she was. Jason's probably. Making the same mistakes Eden and Archie had made. Eden pulled the engagement pebble out from the bottom of her drawers. She rolled it over in her hands, stroking its smooth sides. Her back fell onto her bed, holding the pebble tightly in her palms. Maybe if she held tight enough, he would come back?

Twelve

Eden wanted to skip the next *Here to Help* meeting. She couldn't face it, she couldn't face what people might say. The two reasons she would go would be to see Loren, who messaged her daily, and Camille, who in Eden's eyes, was the most beautiful person to ever grace the earth.
That morning, Eden woke up, showered, but with no hallucinations, and had breakfast. She hadn't seen Juliet in four days, not even on the streets, but then New York was a big city. Eden wanted to text her, or even call her, but now wasn't the right time. Her hair was pulled back into a tight ponytail, it almost pulled the brains out of her; it was that tight. She picked up her bag and looked at herself in the mirror. It was dusty, but her reflection stood in front of her. She didn't like what she saw, so she opened the door and left the apartment.
Eden pushed the door to the community hall she had been to only once before. The walls were decorated with rainbows and things that were supposed to make you

happy. To some degree, it did make her smile, but that didn't distract her from the real reason she was there.
'Eden!' Camille walked up to her, her arms spread wide begging for some sort of affection. Eden hugged her. She smelt like a loaf of fresh bread. Maybe she had just been to the bakery or something like that? It was a nice smell, Eden didn't complain. Camille looked stunning, she always did. Her skin glowed like when the sun hits the top of the ocean and bounces off creating an irresistible light that everyone is drawn to. Camille welcomed everyone with open arms. She was the kindest, most beautiful and empathetic person Eden had met. Camille was wearing a yellow dress that fell to her ankles. Only Camille could pull that off, Eden thought. She had tried to wear yellow before, it didn't look good. Perhaps yellow just wasn't a colour that blonde people should wear.
'You look good, how are you?' Camille asked as she looked Eden up and down.
'I'm good thanks,' Eden lied.
'Amazing, here take a seat, we're about to start.' Camille pulled up a chair for Eden. Each chair was painted a different colour and on the seat was painted an animal that colour. Her's was black, and on it, she had a black panther. Of all the chairs, she had been given the one that wasn't even painted a proper colour. She remembered her conversation with Ezra. Black wasn't a real colour. Typical. This was karma for trying to prove to him that black wasn't a real colour. Maybe it was after all.
Loren sat next to her. She had on her permanent smile, the one which she put on to show how confident she was.

Jealousy was an understatement. Why couldn't Eden be like that, permanently.

'I hope you've all had a great week,' Camille started off saying. A few more people walked in through the door and took a colourful chair. A brown one, an indigo one, and a mint green one. What animal was mint green? She couldn't see what was on the chair. Probably some type of poisonous frog. They were all kinds of colours.

'Why don't we go around and say one thing that we've enjoyed doing this week.' Camille turned to the person next to her. His name was Zach, he wore glasses and oversized shirts and tshirts.

'Um, I baked a cake for my dad, he turned fifty the other day. We had a quiet party with a few friends. I haven't actually been to a party in years, so it was definitely a significant moment, and I enjoyed it, plus the cake was really nice,' Zack finished saying. He spoke quietly, his voice was low, and his mouth barely moved. Eden just wanted a slice of that cake.

There were four more people until it got to her. The problem was, Eden hadn't done anything exciting that week, apart from meet Ezra, and she couldn't say that, not in front of Camille. That was not part of her advice she had given last week.

Three people. Someone had just explained how the most exciting thing they had done that week was walk their dog around Central Park. How boring was their life?

Two people. Someone got their driving licence. That was mildly exciting, now they could escape whenever they wanted to.

One person. He had just been offered a job at a cafe down the road. Maybe Eden could now get half price coffee if she became friendly with this person?
All eyes turned to Eden. She took a gulp and looked up into the circle. She hated the feeling of people staring at her, she hated being the centre of attention. That was rich, a year ago all she wanted was the spotlight.
'I... I decorated my apartment, it needed redoing. I find it quite therapeutic,' she said into the circle. It was very therapeutic destroying lamp shades and ripping up pictures of your ex best friend. Camille smiled at Eden and moved to look at Loren, who explained how she had won some sort of poetry competition she had entered. The talking was over, for now.
After Loren there were six more people, none of them very interesting. This was a group of people, where a lot of them had social anxiety, so the most interesting thing really was then one where someone walked their dog around Central Park.
'I'm glad to hear that all of you have been getting up to some interesting things this week, I can't wait to hear about your week next time we meet.' Camille smiled and stood up.
'I was thinking, who would be interested in sort of a February version of secret santa? We put our names into a hat and then buy a gift for the person we pick out. A Valentines secret santa,' Camille explained. The circle nodded. It wouldn't be too bad of an idea, Eden thought. She only knew Loren, maybe this was the perfect way to branch out and meet even more people.

Eden picked out someone called Devon. She looked around the circle and tried to remember who he was. He sat on the opposite side to her and hardly ever spoke. A bit like Eden then. There wasn't much to infer from what he looked like, maybe she could just buy him a box of chocolates and that could be it. He weaved his thumbs in and out of one another and blinked, a lot. She didn't talk to him, that would give the whole point of the exercise away. After she had given him her crappy present, then she would talk.
'Who'd you get?' Loren tapped Eden's shoulder and grinned excessively.
'I'm not saying,' Eden answered and brought her finger up to her lips.
'That's clearly a sign that you've got me. I'll tell you mine if you tell me yours.' Loren tried to grab the small piece of paper with Devon's name on from Eden's hand. She quickly moved her hand and Loren gave in.
'I got Devon,' Eden sighed and glanced over at him, who was slumped on the orange chair staring into nothing.
'He's so weird, but kinda cute.' Loren followed Eden's eyes over to look at him. He was now picking his nails.
'So… who'd you get?' Eden asked.
'I got Zach. I'm kinda annoyed, he seems like such a geek. Maybe I'll just get him a dictionary or something,' Loren replied and shrugged.
'I've got loads of old vintage style books at my place, you should come over and choose one. I don't mind getting rid of one,' Eden said. Technically they weren't hers to give

away, they were Juliet's, but Juliet wouldn't notice. She might not ever notice.
'Sure, that sounds amazing. Thanks,' Loren added.
Eden picked up one of the cupcakes that was on offer to eat. She actually couldn't remember the last time she ate a cupcake. The hot chocolate was watery and disgusting, but she drank it anyway. Camille put so much time and effort into making everything perfect she felt she couldn't just leave it. Eden caught Camille's yellow dress in the corner of her eye, she was walking towards her.
'Do you want to talk?' Camille asked. No, was the truthful answer. Anything but talking would be nice. She finished her drink and threw it in the bin, then turned to face Camille.
'Yeah sure,' she smiled, fake obviously. Eden followed to the corner of the hall. It was dark and smelled different to what it was like in the middle.
'I was just checking in on you, to see how you've been since the last time we spoke,' Camille explained. She always sat up straight, her posture was immaculate, compared to Eden's slouched over depressed stance.
'Have you acted on any of the advice I gave you last week?' She asked.
Obviously not.
'Yes, I gave him a call, and we've planned to meet up tomorrow,' Eden lied. It was her only way out of this.
Lying.
'That's great to hear.' Camille placed her palm on Eden's leg and leaned forward to smile.

'Do you have an idea of what you're going to do?' She asked again. Eden's mind raced of possible activities she could do on her imaginary get together with her ex boyfriend.

'We're going for a walk, around a park probably,' Eden lied again. She was getting good at this.

'I'm so glad to hear that you're finally coming face to face with the thing you've been so afraid of for so long,' she exclaimed. Eden felt a wave of guilt pass through her. Camille was trying so hard to make Eden happy, when really it just made everything worse. Eden wanted Archie more than anyone. She wanted his voice, his smile, his embrace, his love. And she couldn't have it. She wasn't facing Archie at all.

'Thank you,' was all Eden could say.

'But how are you? What have you been up to this week?' Camille liked her questions clearly.

Apart from two breakdowns, exiling her best friend, meeting someone who was Archie's doppelganger and destroying her apartment, she was fine. Just fine.

'It's been an interesting week. I actually met with Loren the other day, which was nice, and I've just been working in Shore's Records most of the time.' Her voice was shy, she didn't like talking. Correction. She hated talking, especially about her. She wanted to loosen her ponytail, it was too tight. It pulled on her scalp so hard that she was actually getting a headache. Eden could feel herself sweating under her many layers of clothing. She was uncomfortable.

'I love Shore's, I didn't know you worked there? When's your next shift?' Camille smiled. Eden had never noticed how bright her teeth were, maybe because she had never talked to someone literally in pitch black and the only light shining was that of their teeth. Eden had zoned out, she was looking over her shoulder and the few people left in the hall. Devon on his chair, Loren who was refilling her drink with the watery hot chocolate, and Zach who was looking out of the window.

'Tomorrow,' she smiled back at Camille.

'Maybe I'll pop in and say hi.'

Eden didn't know how to reply, so she just smiled, like she always did. It was the safest option.

The walk home was gentle and fresh. She let the few drops of rain fall onto her face and slightly smudge the little makeup she was wearing. The bottom of her jeans had a rim of water around them where she had stepped in a puddle and the water had splashed up above her. When she got home Juliet still hadn't returned. Eden's face dropped. It had been four days, four days too many.

The room was cold, she wrapped herself up in a blanket and fell onto the sofa turning the TV on, and then back off again. Archer King was on. She didn't want to see it. And then she did. Eden turned the TV back on and watched the interview. He wore a dark blue suit, Eden always thought dark blue was his best colour, it made his eyes shine. She turned up the volume so she could hear what was being said. He was tapping his foot to the ground, his knee was bouncing up and down. Eden knew that he always did that when he was nervous. What was he to be nervous about?

He stopped speaking and moved to the stage where he picked up his guitar, a black one with a silver strap, and moved towards the microphone. He was about to sing. The guitar started to produce music. Music she recognised. Eden jumped up and fished for his album under her bed. She pulled it out and sat back down. Her finger skimmed the list of songs before stopping at one. Track seven. Eden turned up the volume even more and fixated her eyes on him, on his body, his guitar, his image. She listened to the song as if it was the first time she had heard it. She let the lyrics swim into her ears, through her brain, down her throat and into her stomach. She let it soak its way into her lungs, her heart and melt into her bones. His face was sweating, it made her sweat. She closed her eyes, and then opened them. He was there, in front of her, the very first time she heard that song. They sat on her bed, his guitar sat on his knees as he strummed the strings carefully with his fingers. She had tears in her eyes, she had tears everywhere. Archie's voice was the most calming voice she had ever heard. It did something to her. Eden wanted to reach out and touch him, but she resisted. She let him sing.
The song ended. Eden hugged the album cover and stared at the TV longingly.
'Archer King with *Loving Someone Like You,* we'll be back after the break,' the interviewer said into the camera. Archie hugged him before the show finished and Eden turned the TV off.

Eden dreamt of cosmic love. A love with so much emotion and so much significance it becomes amazingly unique and special. She still believed in cosmic love. That was her problem.

Thirteen

Her eyes were dark and smoky. She had attempted to do this sultry sort of eyeshadow look for the party Ezra had invited her to. She was already late, but people surely wouldn't miss her. Eden didn't bother dressing up, she didn't want to look like she had made an effort, that would be showing off. Her jeans were light blue and cuffed at the bottom, where she wore her black boots that she had bought back in highschool. Her top was black as well with a white collar that stuck out around her neck. Ezra kept texting her asking where she was. She didn't reply to any of them.
She took the subway, the rain was too heavy for her to walk in, not that she had anything to mess up, her hair was already messy. When wasn't it? As she walked up the stairs to the surface she was greeted with a man, he looked old and desperate. He had a handful of heart shaped balloons that were attached to white or pink ribbons. The man smiled in a freakishly creepy way that

she didn't like. She felt he was hypnotising her with his strange happiness.
'Care for a balloon for your special someone?' He asked as she surfaced the streets. She glanced over at him, his pink suit was lined with gold glitter on the sleeves.
'No thank you.' She continued walking. He followed her.
'Not even a small one, make your valentine the happiest person alive,' he exclaimed. It was Valentine's Day tomorrow. The day she had been dreading the most. Eden had crossed it out of her calendar, she'd tried to block it out of her mind, like it didn't even exist. But that didn't stop everyone else from enjoying it. Eden looked up at the balloons. Some were pink, some were red, some were purple, but all were shaped as a heart. She didn't like the look of this man, he was suspicious, but she knew he wasn't leaving until she bought something.
'I'll take that one.' Eden pointed up at a red one. It was small. Good. She didn't want to be carrying around a massive balloon across the streets of New York. He handed her the balloon, and she handed him the money. What was she going to do with it now?
Eden knew when she arrived because there were birthday balloons surrounding the door. Her heart one wouldn't fit in, she'd have to give it in person.
The place was warm as soon as she was let in. It was filled with lights of all shapes and sizes. And different colours too. There were lamps on practically every square inch of the floor. Eden liked it. She liked light. There were more people then she expected. Clearly a few friends and family to Ezra was a whole community to Eden. He was

there, dressed in black trousers and a red polo shirt which Eden thought was slightly too tight for him. She giggled when she saw him in it.

'You came!' He exclaimed and embraced her in a hug. She wasn't sure where to put her hands as she had her bag in one and the annoying red balloon in the other. 'Is this...?' He pointed at the balloon.

'Oh some weird street seller made me buy one. I thought I'd just leave it here with the other balloons,' she laughed. Eden slipped off her coat and placed it on a nearby chair, along with her bag.

Most of the people there were in the living room. It was decorated with more balloons of various colours and a banner that was strung up across the fireplace.

'Here, I'll introduce you to my mother.' Ezra took Eden's hand and led her through the door to the living room. She was slightly overwhelmed at the people looking at her. Did Ezra never bring a girl home? There were people heavily dressed up in dinner jackets, or dressed up in long flowy dresses. Mainly the older people. Ezra looked like the youngest there until Eden arrived. She felt she was slightly underdressed. No, not slightly, very underdressed. Her jeans looked like trash compared to everyones smart, neat attire. Eden followed Ezra through the crowd of people, ducking out of the way as people welcomed others with open arms.

'Mum, this is Eden,' Ezra said and tapped his mom's shoulder so that she turned around to face them. She was pretty. That was Eden's first thought. Her hair was almost turning grey, but not just yet. It was blonde and reflected light that bounced on it. Eden was incredibly jealous.

'Eden, it's so lovely to meet you. I'm Cindy, Ezra's mother.' She spoke as posh as an American could. No wrinkles appeared when she spoke. That was something to be proud of.

'Would you like a drink?' Cindy pointed to the table behind her loaded with drinks. Mostly alcoholic.

'Do you have any non-alcoholic drinks?' Eden asked and turned to Ezra. He nodded and led her behind his mum to the drinks.

'Here, you like coke?' He pulled out a can from the bucket of ice. Eden took it and smiled. It was cold on her hand, but that's what made it taste so nice. She sighed as she glanced out over everyone, she didn't fit in. Not here.

'There's so many people here,' Eden said as they walked through the crowd of people and found two empty chairs to sit on.

'I know. Imagine if I didn't invite you, I'd have to spend the entire evening with a bunch of fifty year olds,' he answered. Eden laughed. She liked it when he made her laugh. Just like Archie used to do.

'I haven't been to a party in so long,' she admitted. Eden couldn't remember the last time she had been to a party, maybe her eighteenth two December's ago?

'I'm not one for going to big events either, not that this is big. I just prefer to be alone, lying on my bed and crying at the most tragic movies.' Ezra was quiet under the music being played from the speaker on the other side of the room. Eden smiled into his eyes and brushed the loose

curls that had fallen in front of his eyes away. Just like she did to Archie. But this was Ezra. Eden pulled her hand back quickly and bit her lip, gulping as she realised what she had just done. She finished her drink and placed the empty can on the table besides her
'I didn't realise you came from a wealthy family,' Eden said. She looked around again at the people who had been invited. Each one of them she felt could tell a different story about their lives, they were all so proper and posh and incredibly sophisticated. Even in their stance she could see they were well mannered. They all looked the same as his mum though, old and rich.
'My mom's a lawyer and my dad's a doctor. A typical match if you ask me,' he sighed and wrapped his arm around Eden. She sat there tense as he did so. Did they know about the two of them? She looked to her left at his hand and then to him and smiled.
'Thank you for inviting me. I've been so stuck in that apartment recently, I just needed to get out and have fun.' Eden started to regret wearing any eyeshadow at all. She felt embarrassed that he wasn't looking into her real eyes. Then, would she really want him to?
'You don't have to tell me, I've only known you a week, but has anything happened to you recently? You seem… uptight. Maybe this is just the real you, I've never been in a relationship before, forget I asked.' He turned away briefly, embarrassed to say the least.
'No it's fine,' she turned his head to face her again. She was embarrassed for letting him believe this relationship

was actually going to last. He didn't know it was a rebound, but she did.

'I've just had some ups and downs with a friend, that's all.' She was technically telling the truth. Her and Juliet were non-existent at the moment. And so was Archie.

'Clearly I met you at the right time then.' He kissed her cheek. Again, she froze. She wasn't sure how to react, so she just smiled and let him look into her fake, made up eyes.

Eden let Ezra go and talk to some of the other guests, he couldn't just stay and talk to her the whole evening. Well, he could, but she didn't want him to. She wanted to go to the bathroom and take off her makeup. She hated it now, it made her look like a panda she thought. She didn't want to look like a panda.

The bathroom was at the back of the living room. She'd have to make her way through the crowd and try to not talk to anyone. Eden hung her head low and watched her feet as she winded in and out of the people. She could see the bathroom door. It was shut. Someone was already in there. Eden stopped and looked behind her, and then back at the bathroom door. She waited, but not too close, she didn't want to make it seem that she was desperate for the bathroom. She didn't even need it, she just wanted to take off the goddamn awful eye makeup she thought looked so cool an hour ago. The hum of people talking in the background stopped and the lights were turned off, apart from one, the small lamp in the corner where Eden and Ezra had been sitting. Everyone suddenly started singing *Happy Birthday* to Cindy. Eden felt obliged to join in. Whoever was in the bathroom was missing out. She mumbled the words to the song and watched Ezra bring in a cake stacked with pink and gold candles. How she could tell what colour they were she did not know. Cindy clapped her hands together and smiled at her Ezra. He was smiling too, and that made Eden smile. But she still wanted to get rid of the eyeshadow that she had painted on her eyes. She heard the door behind her open, but she didn't turn around, not yet. She wanted to watch Cindy blow out the candles and make a wish. Eden always wondered why people made wishes on their birthday. They nearly never came true. Maybe it's just an in the moment tradition that people do.

Eden shut the door to the bathroom and flicked the switch to turn on the light. The bathroom was big, and it was neat. The walls were painted turquoise and one wall had gold stripes going down it as well. There were pots of plants in each corner, even on the windowsill above the bath. There was a bath on the ground floor bathroom? Eden just wanted to see what was in the other bathrooms now. She walked over to the mirror, it had those lights attached to it which Eden had always wanted to have. She turned the tap on and let the water run until it was warm. Eden hated cold water.

She splashed the water up into her eyes and rubbed vigorously, determined to take it all off. What made her want to put it on in the first place? This wasn't her. She never wore makeup. It wasn't like she was even trying to impress anyone. Eden looked back up at herself in the mirror, and was greeted by a blinding light from the shine the mirror was giving off. Maybe she didn't want a mirror with lights on after all now.

She really did look like a panda now. The makeup had smudged all the way down her cheeks. Eden rubber at her entire face now, the rest of her makeup started to drip off into the sink. There was a whirlpool of neutral colours in front of her eyes, mixing with the water. Her face was dripping wet and looked like a painted canvas that had gone wrong. What had she done? It looked better when she looked like a panda before smudging. Eden just wanted to wash off everything, the hurt, the anger, the pain. Maybe if she scrubbed hard enough she could.

Her phone buzzed from the back pocket of her jeans. Eden dried her hands on the white towel, that was now not so white, more of a light grey. She pulled out her phone and scanned the message. Eden didn't care what she looked like, she needed to get home, now. Ezra was talking to his mom, again.

'I've got to go, I'm really sorry.' She kissed his cheek.

'Wait, what's all over your face? Were you crying?' He asked, concerned. Ezra followed Eden into the corridor where she slid her coat on and swung her bag over her shoulder.

'No, I'm fine, really. I just really need to get home, sorry,' she replied and tried to dry her blackened face with her coat sleeve.

'Well let me take you home,' he pointed to his coat hanging on the end of the stairs.

'No, no you should stay, but it's been really nice, thank you for inviting me,' she was breathless, but she continued speaking, 'I'll call you later, and tell your mum I said thank you and happy birthday.'

Eden opened the door and waved goodbye, Ezra smiled and waved a little, and then watched her walk down the stairs and onto the street. He watched her go, before running out into the rain and spinning her round. He pressed his lips onto hers and let the rain run through his neatly hairsprayed hair. She laughed as they parted.

'What was that for?' She asked and dug her hands into the pockets of her coat.

'Happy Valentine's, for tomorrow, I guess?' He lifted his shoulders up and down. His red polo shirt was darkening as the rain poured on it. He could hardly open his eyes through the rain, it splashed onto his eyelashes and into his eyes, which Eden thought was adorable. Adorable, that was her and Archie's word. Shit.

'I've really got to go,' Eden whispered after they had stood there for a minute looking into each other's eyes.

'Right, yes, sorry.'

'Don't be sorry,' she brought her hand up to his head and brushed her fingers through his wet hair. She kissed him. She had to stop kissing him without him knowing the truth.

'I'll see you tomorrow?' He questioned. She nodded and turned around to walk away, for real this time. He watched her and then ran back up the stairs to the party. Eden looked over her shoulder, but he wasn't there, he had gone back inside.

She got back home covered in rainwater. She was pretty sure the makeup she had tried to take off had been washed away with the rain. The apartment was cold and dark, apart from one room. She could see the kitchen light had been turned on. Eden walked in and sat down at the table. Juliet was there, holding a cup of coffee in her hands.

'What happened to your eyes?' Juliet asked. Clearly the rain hadn't washed it all off.

'Oh,' Eden rubbed at her eyes even more, 'long story.' Eden looked down at her feet, she didn't know what to say. She wanted to let Juliet speak first. Juliet was looking at the floor too. Awkward was an understatement.

'Eden I'm sorry,' Juliet finally said. She looked up at Eden, who was still staring at her feet.

'I shouldn't've said those things, I was angry and annoyed and…'

'No you weren't.' Eden spoke. Eden could see Juliet was about to cry, there were tears welling up in her eyes.

'What do you mean?' Juliet replied. She had let her hair loose and was wearing clothes Eden had never seen before. So she had bought new clothes then.

'You weren't angry, you have nothing to be angry at, so don't say you were angry.'

'Eden…' Juliet started saying.

'Juliet you have this perfect life, you're getting a degree, you have the perfect boyfriend, you have this amazing apartment. If anything, you're angry at me, for coming in and ruining your perfect little life you had set up.' Eden could feel the rage inside of her burning up, it was like a fire had just been started and she was letting it all go.

'Eden that's not true,' Juliet looked up and tried to reach out for Eden's hand. She pulled away quickly.

'I think deep down you know it is.' Eden stood up and started to leave the room.
'Wait where are you going?' Juliet called after her. She had tears falling down her face like when rain falls down a window.
'I think it's time I leave,' Eden began.
'Well, can we pick this up tomorrow then?' But Juliet didn't realise what Eden meant.
'No, I think it's time for me to leave, permanently.'
Juliet followed Eden through to her bed. She was desperate. She was shaking like she was cold, maybe she was, Eden couldn't tell.
The rain outside beat down on the windows, it was loud, louder than normal. Eden could imagine it applauding her for coming face to face with what Juliet thought. Juliet was angry, she was angry that she let Eden live in her apartment, eat her food, and then kick her out of her own apartment. But Juliet didn't show it. She never showed it. That's why Eden clung onto her for so long, because Juliet was the best actor she had ever met.
'Eden you don't know what you're doing,' Juliet tried to grab hold of Eden's arm, which was frantically stuffing clothes into a bag. 'Eden, stop, it's your mind telling you that you need to leave, but you don't. Sit down, we need to talk, Eden!' Juliet's fist collided with Eden's face. Both of them fell back onto the wooden floor. There was blood dripping from Eden's mouth, bright red blood the colour of strawberry jam. She brought her hand up to her mouth to stop the bleeding and looked into Juliet's eyes. She was breathing heavily, Eden could see her chest pounding up

and then down and then up again. Her eyes were full of tears, real ones, the ones that tasted like salt as some of them escaped into your mouth. And then Eden realised she was wrong, and this time Juliet would never forgive her.

Fourteen

When Eden woke up the next morning she was still in her bed. Whatever happened last night she wanted to move on from, but she didn't know if Juliet wanted the same. Her lip was throbbing with pain, it looked like she had tried to swallow a tennis ball but it had got lodged in her mouth instead. Eden brought her hand up to touch it, and immediately pulled away. It hurt to even touch.
She reached over to her phone to see if Ezra had called, or texted, or sent her a funny GIF to make her laugh. Crap. She had forgotten to put it on charge overnight. The cable was swung behind her lamp, the one she hadn't smashed. She plugged her phone in and lay back on her bed looking up at the vacant ceiling. Juliet was up, she could hear movement in the kitchen, but she just couldn't face going in at the moment. The smell of coffee begged her to move, but she didn't. Eden thought about never leaving that bed again, maybe it would be for the best.

Eden hadn't even changed from last night. Her legs were still plastered into the jeans she had worn and there were black stains all over the white collar of the top where she had tried to scrub off the black eye makeup she had put on.. Her boots were flung across the room, one by the TV and the other next to her bed. She could hear humming coming from the kitchen, and wasn't sure whether to take it as a good sign or a bad sign. Eden's head was spinning from last night, she hadn't drunk a single drop of alcohol yet she felt like she had just woken up with the worst hangover she could imagine. It felt like a builder was smashing away at the insides of her brain and pulling them all out in a long line. Or like someone was stamping on her head and she couldn't move because she was so frozen in fear of getting hurt and feeling more pain.
She lay there a little longer, contemplating life and what she was doing in it. It was her most frequent activity, apart from breaking down and crying daily. Or were they the same thing? They sure seemed like it in the moment.
'Hey.' Juliet walked in, fully dressed in Eden's favourite green skirt and white top combination that Juliet wore. She carried a tray filled with food, a plate of pancakes decorated with strawberries and blueberries and maple syrup, a slice of toast and a mug of hot coffee. Eden sat up in her bed.
'Thank you,' she reached out to take the tray. It smelled even better when it was right in front of her. Everything about it screamed *I'm sorry, please forgive me.*
Juliet hovered over Eden awkwardly, she danced her fingers in and out of one another and looked at the wall in

front of her. Part of Eden wanted to slap her across the face because she wanted her to feel the exact pain she was in at that moment, but the other half wanted to just forgive her, so that they could go back to being their goofy self.

'Sit,' Eden moved her legs to the left of her and pointed to where she wanted Juliet to sit. Juliet froze, stared at the space on the bed, then sat down carefully right on the edge.

'How's your lip? Do you want some more pain killers?' Juliet pointed at Eden's face and tilted her head.

'I think I'll be fine,' she brushed her fingers against the swelling, and then picked up the coffee and brought it to her mouth. It stung a little as the coffee hit her lips, but she got over the pain. It wasn't the most painful thing she had experienced in her life.

'Do you want to talk about what happened?' Juliet asked. Eden thought she was shaking, or maybe she was just nervous. Her leg bounced up and down as she sat on the edge of the bed and the hairs on her arm stuck straight up. Eden shook her head as she took another mouthful of pancake. She finished chewing what was in her mouth and you could see the food go down her throat as she gulped.

'I was wrong, you were just trying to help. I guess I've just turned a blind eye to everyone that's trying to look out for me.' Eden tucked her hair behind her ears. Juliet liked it when she did that, she could finally see her whole face without it being hidden behind her hair.

'You can't blame yourself for everything Eden, you're not the only person to mess things up in their life.' Juliet pulled both legs up onto the bed and crossed them so she was facing Eden. 'You've just got to figure out what's worth fighting for, and follow it, otherwise you'll be in ten different battles and lose all of them.'
'I know… I know.'
There was a silence, and the rain stopped. Eden knew the rain had stopped for two reasons:
1. Something inside of her escaped, like the rain cloud. There was no rain cloud in her anymore, no reason for it to rain.
2. She could hear the few birds that flew around New York. She could never usually hear them, because the rain was so much stronger than all of the other noise. She liked hearing the birds.

Eden tried to look in front of her, but the brightness of the sun had already met her eyes before she could look at Juliet. She could tell Juliet was smiling, she could sense it.
'Eden know that whatever happens, I'm here for you. No matter how hard you try to block me out, I'm always going to be here. We're like swallows that always return to their safe space. You're my safe space, you always have been. And there's no storm that can blow me away from you.'
Eden found it kind of cringe, but it was true. Her face had flushed and her cheeks were coloured pink. It made her look more alive, which at this point, was something she wanted. She pictured the swallows flying back from wherever they were born, they travelled across the world, and they always returned.

'When did you learn about swallows migrating?' Eden laughed as she had a mouthful of food.
'I couldn't say if I knew.' She smiled. Her smile was one of those smiles that made you forget all of the bad things going on. She was a walking talking sunshine. Why couldn't everyone be like that?
'I'm going to meet Jason, but I'll be back later.' Juliet stood up and went back into the kitchen, and then her room. Eden watched her get ready, and then leave the apartment, and she was all by herself again.
The pancakes were delicious, she hadn't had a proper breakfast in days, partly because Juliet did the cooking, and Eden did the eating. Her head had stopped throbbing continuously, there was just a small ongoing pain at the back of her head now.
She got changed, her outfit choices were never extravagant, she didn't want to stick out. Her jeans were probably a shade darker than what she was wearing yesterday, a real change in her eyes. Eden pulled out a top from the bottom of her drawer. It was pink, her favourite shade of pink. Correction. Archie's favourite shade of pink. Archie's favourite top.

Archie had kept his promise. The two of them went to California that summer, but they didn't drive. Eden's mom had straight up refused to let the two of them drive all by themselves from Iowa to California and back. *It's dangerous and not safe* is what she would say whenever they asked, so they booked the cheapest flights they could find.

'So where are we actually going? Eden tugged at Archie's arm as they walked out of the airport and into a taxi. Archie had kept everything a secret from her, what they were doing, where they were going. She was desperate to find out. Everyone there, she thought, had souls of sunshine, because they always seemed so beautifully placed in the world. They looked like God had just dropped off his most perfect people into California and told them to never leave.
'Not long now.' He placed their suitcases in the back of the taxi and kissed her forehead, before talking to the driver quietly so that Eden couldn't hear them. She tried to listen in, but they were too good.
Eden had never been to California before. She imagined it to be full of celebrities and beaches and people who had thousands of followers on Instagram and posed for photos in every location possible. Most of it was true. The windows were open and she could already feel the hot sun melting onto her pale skin. Archie wrapped his arm around her shoulder and she leaned against him. Her eyes were so close to shutting and letting her sleep, but she couldn't miss out on the sights. The air conditioning blew onto her face, she liked it. The smell of salty water refreshed her, it was her new favourite smell.
They pulled up outside a hotel, it looked small and well looked after. The walls were white washed and had green vines climbing up the sides like in Jack and the Beanstalk. There was a blue door that looked like it needed repainting. There was paint peeling off it and a pile of

already fallen flakes that had been swept together, but not yet collected.
Eden looked up at Archie, he was smiling broadly. He pulled out their bags and took Eden's hand, walking her into the hotel. They were in Malibu, right on the beach. She could see the sea through various windows, she just wanted to jump in it and relax.
'This was the hotel I came to the first time I came to California, it made me fall in love with the place,' Archie said as they waited in the lobby. There were seashells strung up on the walls and old fishing nets were draped from the ceiling. Potted plants lined the floor and there were pictures in black and white of old sailors and events that had happened in the area. She clung onto Archie's shoulder as her eyes wandered the room and took everything in.
'It's perfect. I love it.' She replied to him.
They were shown to their room, it was small, and decorated the same as the lobby. Old barrels were used as bedside tables, and there were seashells painted blue and yellow stuck to the walls. Their room walked straight out onto the beach. Eden just wanted to lie on the sand, swim in the water and relax. It was all she wanted.
The water was gentle as she waded in, the sunset like orange on a painted blue canvas. The water was soft and clean. Gentle. She waded in even further until it reached above her hips and her fingers were dipped in. Waves of deep blue creeped towards her and then faded out behind her. Gentle. It was bluer than she had imagined it. It wasn't the blue colour you would use to colour in the sea,

it was deeper and more real. It wasn't fake like a colouring pencil. And there wasn't a definitive line where the ocean met the sky, it was blurred together. It wasn't a five year olds picture that was hung up on the fridge for years, it was a painting that would be on display for generations. The sea would always be there, it was never leaving. The ocean breathed, rising and falling with musical ease. It became her pulse, rushing through her veins and into her heart. They were syncopated in rhythm, rising and falling like the sun. She had never experienced something like it. Archie wrapped his arms around her bare waist. His skin was wet and smooth, she felt connected as their skin touched. He made kisses down her neck, moving her sea soaked hair to make room. There was always room for Archie. She could smell the freshness of the air in him.
'I wish we could stay here, forever,' she whispered into his ear.
'Follow me.' He took her hand and led her out of the water and onto the sand. It stuck to their feet and crawled up their ankles, Eden had always wanted that to happen. She wanted the feeling of having sand stuck to your feet, she'd seen it in movies before.
He led her up the stairs and into their room and sat her down on the bed, wrapped in a towel that was decorated with embroidered starfish. Their room had day old empty bottles and clothes thrown across the floor. Eden dried herself off and threw on one of the tops that had found its way halfway across the floor. A pink one, her favourite shade of pink. Archie stared at her, in love.

'I like that top, it's beautiful,' he said. He picked up his guitar he had lugged all the way from Iowa and placed it on his knee. He looked cold, the water could probably freeze on his body. Eden stood up and wrapped her towel around him, and then sat in front of him. His warmth warmed her up, she was filled with these bubbles of warmth and happiness. There was nothing she wanted more.

Eden thought it was a blessing to hear Archie play his songs. It was her own mini personal concert just for her. She listened to him playing, she listened to the waves crashing the surface in the distance, she listened to the birds, the children playing on the beach. She listened to everything, because that was what she loved. When she listened she understood the world better, her eyes were opened.

His song faded out into the distance and she sat there humming.

'Eden,' Archie spoke. She opened her eyes, she didn't realise she had closed them. 'Are you okay?' He asked softly. Salt had dried just where his hairline started, it looked like he had a halo of white light circling his head. Eden wiped it away and stroked the side of his face as she brought her hand back down to her lap.

'Yeah, I'm fine.' She looked up into his eyes. He had moved and was kneeling right in front of her, breathing down her neck. She reached up and pressed her lips against his, tasting the salt from the sea water that he hadn't wiped away yet. The towel fell from his shoulders and he cupped her face in his hands. He was gentle around her, it was his guilty pleasure. She held him tighter, kissing him harder like it was the only thing to hold on to. And then they were lying on the floor, their bodies pressed against one another, and breathing gently into each other. His arm was wrapped around her waist and his fingers played with the frills on the bottom of her pink top. He liked that pink top, a lot.

Eden held the pink top in her hands and played with the frills that lined the hem. She hadn't worn it since. She studied every inch of it, each lace detail, everything. Eden slipped off the top she was wearing and pulled the pink one on over her head. It was loose around the sides, she had lost weight, too much of it, since she last wore it. The mirror reflected back perfectly, it was still the same colour pink. His favourite pink.

She went to work wearing that pink top, for some reason she felt safe in it. And then she remembered it was Valentine's Day and she started to regret wearing pink. Recently Eden regretted wearing a lot of things, maybe she should just stick to wearing black everyday.

'You look nice today Eden,' Mr Shore exclaimed as she walked in through the door and set her bag down under the counter.

'Thanks, Happy Valentine's by the way,' she added. Someone should say it to him.

'It's been a long time since someone's said that to me,' he joked, but Eden knew it was true. He was old, a widower, and alone. He treated Eden like his daughter most of the time.

'I like what you've done with the place,' Eden pointed out the few Valentine's decorations that were strung up around the store and in the windows. Red and pink bunting in the shape of a heart draped from the ceilings above them, and there was a heart drawn onto the window with window paint.

'Every year I decorate the place. I like making people feel happy and loved. Here look,' Shore pointed at the basket on the counter filled with heart shaped chocolates and cookies he had made the night before.

'I'll be sure to take some if there's any left over,' she laughed.

'You better take some now, I always sell out of these!' Eden stuffed a bag of cookies into her bag below and looked around the store. It was going to be a busy day. But she couldn't stop thinking about Archie, and his beautiful eyes, and his beautiful smile. She tried to picture what he would look like if he saw her wearing the pink top. He could leave her life, but he couldn't leave her soul. That's not how it works when you fall in love. You fell in love for a reason, you can't just stop loving someone because it ended. She knew that deep down, somewhere, he still loved her. Because when you fall in love, they don't just say it because it sounds nice, you really do fall in love. You just hope that someone will be there to catch you, because otherwise you're just going to keep on falling. Her heart beat fast as she pulled at the frills on the pink top, hoping that Archie was pulling them too. It would make her the happiest girl in the world to see Archie pulling on the frills just one more time.

When Eden got home Juliet was back, cooking dinner. Eden had missed her freshly cooked meals.
'How's Jason?' Eden asked as she slouched her body down at one of the kitchen chairs. Juliet's hair was high up in a bun and she had wrapped around her an orange apron that Eden had always despised.
'Yeah, fine. We just did some uni work together and then went for a walk. How was Shore's today?' Juliet asked and let the food simmer whilst she sat down and wiped her brow.
'Busy, but nice. I sometimes enjoy the busier days,' she laughed, 'wait, why aren't you having a Valentine's dinner with Jason?'
Juliet smiled, 'because I wanted to spend tonight with my best friend instead. Happy Galentines,' she exclaimed.
'Don't say that, I've never heard of anything more cringe in my life.' They both laughed loudly until there were tears appearing in their eyes.
They made the most of their evening, dancing to embarrassing music and eating until they couldn't physically put any more food into their mouths.
'What's that on your top?' Juliet pointed down at the bottom of Eden's pink top. Eden hadn't realised anything was there. She walked over to the mirror and turned around so she could see the back of it. There was a faint mark on it, a phrase or something.
'Here,' Juliet walked up, knelt down and made out what it said. 'Why would it say *Malibu Hotel?* Is that the brand?' Eden knew why it said that. It was the name of the song he sang for her when she and Archie were there. He had

written on her top the name of the song. Eden turned and reached for the record under her bed again. There it was. The eighth song. *Malibu Hotel.*

Fifteen

'So I was thinking pizza?' Ezra picked up the takeaway menu from his coffee table and passed it to Eden. It was colourful and hurt Eden's eyes, as did most things, apart from Ezra. For some reason he didn't make her ache inside. He soothed her and tried to piece her back together without realising. That's why she was so drawn to him. Because he was the medicine in her world of pain.
'Pizza sounds good,' she glanced over the menu, but she knew what she was having.
'Great, what do you want?' He moved closer to her so that he could see the menu.
'Just a plain cheese one, please.' She smiled, but it wasn't a happy smile. Something was off, and Ezra knew it. Her face was sunken in more that usual and her voice was quiet like she had just lost her voice. She was a mouse in a world of cats.
'You are the most boring person I have ever met,' he said sarcastically. She laughed at herself, but shyly.
Eden sat on Ezra's sofa, in his apartment, but she didn't feel comfortable. She wanted to, she tried to, but the walls

surrounding her felt they were watching her every move. They didn't want her to do anything that would hurt Archie. The place was small, and near his mother's house. The sofa was brown and looked like it had come straight from a flea market or the streets. And it smelled of old people. Not the nice smelling old people either.

'Okay all ordered, it should be here soon.' Ezra walked back over to the sofa and fell next to Eden. She stopped staring at the wooden floorboards and up at him. His face shone like a thousand stars, and yet Eden only saw darkness. She didn't know what to say, so she didn't say anything. Maybe that was the best thing she had ever decided to do. All she did was smile, and wrap his hair around her fingers. The curls fell perfectly in place on them, just like Archie.

'Are you okay?' He cupped her face in the palm of his hand and lifted her chin to look deep into his eyes. Her eyes almost turned black for a minute, or at least that's what he thought he saw.

Her head nodded up and down immediately, it was the worst thing she could've done.

'I'm just thinking,' she answered.

'About what?'

'Life. How it'll be over before we know it, and none of us are very good at stopping to savour it.'

Ezra didn't reply for a moment, he just listened to her voice, replayed it in his head over and over.

'Maybe you should stop thinking so much about savouring it and start living it,' he said.

How could she start living her life without Archie though? She had stopped, and now she couldn't start.
'Maybe I should,' but she knew it was a lie.
With Ezra, Eden tried to be someone she wasn't. A better version of who she was. But you can't pretend to be someone you're not, because pretending is faking, and fakers are always discovered. She couldn't change, because on the inside, she still had the same heart, she breathed the same air, and she thought the same thoughts. She would have to die to become someone new.
Eden placed her head on Ezra's lap, he stroked her hair like he was petting a puppy. She wanted to close her eyes and fall asleep, but Ezra had ordered pizza and planned a beautiful night, and she didn't want to ruin it, for him. She looked at the pictures hanging on the wall in front of her. They were printed photos of Ezra when he was younger, and cuter. He hadn't changed, at least she didn't think he had. He had the same curls in his hair, the same eyes, the same smile for that matter. Your smile can't really change though, it can only get happier.
'How old were you there?' She pointed to the one on the far left, he looked young and was surrounded by people that loved him. He squinted at it.
'Probably around ten, my looks were not the best,' he laughed.
'You look cute, my appearance did not look that good when I was ten.' She sat up and crossed her legs on the sofa, pulling the blanket over her knees.
'Prove it.'

Eden pulled out her phone and started stalking her mum's facebook. If there were any photos of her at ten, she would find them there. She scrolled up, scanning each photo as she did so. There were some of her and Juliet, her and other friends, her on holiday with family, her with grandparents. And her and Archie. She hadn't deleted him. Eden wanted to stop and look at the photos, she wanted to indulge them, but she didn't. Not in front of Ezra.
'Here,' Eden turned the phone to show Ezra. She was at a farm, dressed in a bright green raincoat and yellow boots which were covered in mud from the rain.
'Now that is cute,' he exclaimed.
'I was a fashion icon,' she joked and put her phone back into her pocket.
'I'd like to see you in that outfit.'
'I don't think I'd fit into any of my old clothes.' False. She probably would.
'Follow me,' he pulled her up from the warm spot she had made on the sofa and led her into his room. She hadn't been in there before. The walls were painted head to toe in dark blue paint and there were film posters hung up randomly everywhere. It was a true kids bedroom, but Eden didn't say that. The bed was big and was covered in a black duvet cover. Black was his favourite 'colour'. Eden noticed the glow in the dark stars that were stuck on the ceiling above his head. She really felt as if she had walked into a fourteen year old boys bedroom for the first time. There were piles of unwashed clothes in the corner, Ezra

tried kicking them further away, but it just made Eden laugh.

'That film is amazing,' Eden pointed at one of the film posters hung up on his wall. The Breakfast Club.

'I always wanted to be an Andrew Clark growing up, the athlete kid that was popular. Never worked out though,' he admitted. Ezra had his head in the wardrobe, looking for something clearly.

Eden was Claire Standish, but she didn't want to admit it. She was a Claire turned old Alison. Maybe that's how she should identify herself as now.

'Here,' Ezra threw a green coat onto the bed, followed by a pair of yellow wellington boots. She stood there, confused, and then realised what was going on.

'You want me to recreate my looks from ten years ago?' She asked.

'Yep,' Ezra answered, 'don't worry, I'll do the same.'

'So we're playing dress up?'

'Gosh no not like that! It'll just be fun to recreate old photos,' he exclaimed.

'Fine, hand me the green coat.' She held out her hand and Ezra gave her the coat, it was darker than the one in the picture, and was obviously made for a man. Eden felt like she was destroying the memory of the picture if she recreated it, but this was Ezra's idea, and she didn't want to break any more hearts. The previous one being her own.

She stood in the doorway blocking out the light so you could only see her shadow. The coat fell just above her knees and the yellow boots were far too big for her. She had tried to recreate the hairstyle as well, but her hair was now too short to put it up in two space buns and make them look half decent. In her mind there was dramatic music playing as she stood there, one arm leant against the side of the door, the other fixated to her hip. It was a look.

'Now that is an outfit,' Ezra marveled. He couldn't talk, he was dressed in bright red trousers and a blue jumper that was supposed to say *I'd rather be playing football* but instead it was official Knicks merch. And the shoes he wore topped the look off. Pristine white. She had never seen shoes so white before.

'If we went onto the streets right now we'd be arrested for looking like complete weirdos,' Eden remarked.

'Well we've got to receive our pizza looking like this.'

'You can, I'm not.' Eden started unzipping the green coat, but the zip didn't budge.

'Hey I like my green coat. And on you I like it even better.' She rolled her eyes and tried to unzip it again.

'I look like Shrek,' she huffed.

'My Shrek.'

That made Eden stop. No one had referred to her as *my* before. Not since Archie. Maybe she just wasn't used to the lovey language that people used in a relationship. But she couldn't get it out of her head. Ezra had referred to her as *mine*. She wanted to say it back, but she couldn't. It was like there was a big boulder blocking her from saying it. She wasn't sure if she wanted to say it, ever. Would anyone really be hers? You can't own someone, the only person you can own is yourself.

She just smiled. It was the thing she was best at. Smiling without meaning it.

'Come, the food will be here soon.' He led her back into the living room. She didn't need leading, she was a grown woman, she could show herself to the sofa.

He was right, the food came soon after. He answered the door in his absurd outfit, Eden sat in the background. If anything, the delivery guy was more intrigued with Eden's outfit. Who wouldn't be ? She was wearing a huge green coat and yellow boots. You would think she was overheating, but she was cold. That's why she kept the coat on really.

The pizza tasted like any other pizza. Nice. Eden was grateful that he had bought it, she hadn't had pizza since forever. Since Archie. Forever and Archie were the same thing. He was forever ago, and yet she thought he'd love her forever. That's what he promised.

She wanted to go, so she did. But she kissed Ezra goodbye, or rather he kissed her, but this time she kissed him back. To make him happy. All she ever wanted was to make other people happy. He offered to walk her home, but she said no, she politely declined. Deep down she knew he wanted her to spend the night, they had done it once before. One too many times.

When she got home Ezra texted her.

There's a new movie out, Disney, but I'm a sucker for a happy ending. You wanna go?

Eden read the message, started typing, deleted what she was typing, and then went to sleep.

When she woke he hadn't double texted, but he knew she had seen his message. She wanted to reply, but she couldn't find the words, so she didn't.

She ate breakfast one handed, holding her phone in her hand, her thumb over the keyboard contemplating whether to reply. She didn't. She put the phone down in front of her and ate her breakfast.

She got in the bath, it was warm, she had lit candles like she saw on Pinterest when you searched up aesthetically pleasing bath setups. She closed her eyes and listened to, for the first time ever, classical music. The Piano Sonata No. 14 in C sharp minor, 'Quasi una fantasia', Op 27, No. 2, popularly known as the Moonlight Sonata, by Ludwig van Beethoven. She tried to write her reply in her head, but all she could hear was the music. Maybe it was for the best.

She had Loren over to pick out a book for the stupid gift swap they were doing. The Great Gatsby. She thought of the quote:

>'And in the end, we were all just humans...
>drunk on the idea that love,
>only love,
>could heal our brokenness.'

She was living alongside that quote. Drunk on the idea that Ezra could mend her from Archie, but really it only hurt her even more. She wanted to text Ezra the quote, but she knew she couldn't, so she continued to ignore it.

Even at work she tried to piece together how she could reply. But how could she piece together a reply when she couldn't even piece herself together? So she buried her phone right at the bottom of her bag and tried to move her mind away from it. But what if he walked into the store? How would she reply to him there and then?

She got home, the lights were dimmed, the sky was dark, the rain poured heavily. She played her reply over and over in her head, and then sent it.

Sounds great! Can't wait, send me the deets.

She was a sucker for a happy ending too, but with Archie, not Ezra.

Sixteen

On Tuesday Eden waited out in the rain under the canopy outside the movie theatre. She was glad she hadn't worn white, because if she had, her top would've gone transparent by now. She could see Ezra in the distance, he was waving, but she pretended not to see him. Bless his heart, he was trying so hard. Eden desperately wanted this evening to go well, she couldn't face him asking her if she was okay, again.
'Are you hungry, do you want popcorn?' He asked as he walked her inside. Her hair was sodden in water from walking there, she really should start taking the subway more often.
'I think i'll be fine, I have water in my bag,' she smiled. His face was covered in tiny water droplets which Eden thought were adorable. Adorable, she used to call Archie that.
'Okay, well I'm gonna get some anyway,' he laughed. The movie wasn't going to start for another fifteen minutes, but Eden just wanted to sit down. She waited in line for popcorn with Ezra. He had wrapped his arm around her

shoulder, she wanted to move it, but something inside of her liked being held close to someone, even if it was Ezra. For the entire one hour and fifty two minutes they sat in their seats Ezra had his arm wrapped around her like they were some type of inseparable pair. It was the longest one hour and fifty two minutes of her life, and yet she didn't want to leave. If that was what happiness could feel like, she wished she could never leave her seat again. All she wanted was happiness, and yet all she received was an imploding well of darkness. Eden could smell the strong scent of aftershave he had on, it was nice, and she liked it. A lot. It sat perfectly in the well of his neck where she occasionally rested her head.

They walked out hand in hand, although Eden wished they didn't. Somehow it didn't feel right to hold someone else's hand the way she held Archie's. She felt like she was betraying him.

'So, what are you doing now?' Ezra asked as they entered the streets again.

'I'll probably just go back home, and watch more TV,' she added. When she looked at him she had to lift her head up, because he was gorgeously taller than she was.

'We could grab some dinner, I know a place not too far away.' It was clear Ezra really wanted this. So she said yes, reluctantly, but she didn't show it.

Ezra was right, the food was nice. Some of the nicest food she'd had in a long while. The restaurant was one of those underground types that you wouldn't know existed unless you had been told personally where it was. The walls were naked and had strings of fairy lights hung up all around.

The tables looked like the ones you would find at a flea market or on the side of the street that no one wanted. Maybe they really were. There weren't many people there, enough to call it a restaurant, and enough to be able to order your food and not have it come out immediately because they had nothing else to cook.
Eden watched Ezra eat his food. Some people would find that creepy, but he was so caught up on eating he didn't notice Eden. His black sweater looked like it had just been bought from a vintage shop from the 80s. And there were crumbs that showed up on it too, but not many. Who didn't make at least a handful of crumbs when they ate?
'How did your mother like the *Rumours* album you gave her?' Eden asked in an attempt to start a conversation.
'She loved it, she won't stop listening to it either,' he replied. Ezra wiped his face with a napkin as he finished his food.
'It's funny, I actually never liked Fleetwood Mac before you came in that day,' she confessed.
'What? I thought you loved them.'
'I do now, I went home and listened to all of their songs. And of course I knew some of their songs, like *Songbird*. You can love a song so much, but not like the artist.' Eden smiled wearily. Her voice was quiet over the music being played in the restaurant.
'The fact that you went home and listened to their songs only makes me like you more,' he spoke.
'My heart just grew ten times its size.'
The waiter cleaned their plates, and they were left with an empty table.

'When did you first start listening to *Rumours* then?' Eden asked curiously.

'Probably when I was thirteen maybe fourteen. People thought I was weird because I never listened to the typical cool music,' he explained. Eden felt a sense of sympathy for him when he said it.

'Well, I think you're cool,' she grabbed his wrist that lay on the table in front of her.

The song playing finished and another one started to play. It wasn't a coincidence that the one playing was *Songbird*. Or maybe it was.

'You're kidding right? Did you plan this?' She joked.

'Swear down I didn't.' He put up his hands like he was surrendering and smiled.

'What are the chances?'

He stood up from his seat and walked around to where Eden sat.

'Come on,' he held out his hand like he was about to ask her to dance.

'I'm not dancing, no way is that happening,' she stayed fixed on her chair.

'There's like no one here, no one's going to judge you,' he stated.

'Yeah but what if they do?' She asked.

'I promise you, they won't.'

Eden took his hand and he lifted her up so they were face to face. She wrapped her arms around his neck so that they were slow dancing. Eden could sense the stares they were getting, she wanted to look around, but she didn't. Her eyes were too fixed on Ezra and his face. His curls looked curlier than usual. Had he done something to them? They swayed back and forth to the music, his arms wrapped around her waist, pulling her in closer. The last time she had slow danced was with Archie, and the first time she had slow danced was with Archie.

And when she looked up at Ezra, it wasn't Ezra. Archie was smiling at her. The school hall was filled with other people too, their arms wrapped around their loved one. Balloons lined the walls and music played from the speakers. This was the last back to school dance Eden would go to, and this time, she was going with Archie. His suit was black, and sleek, and he wore a pink bow tie that matched Eden's pink dress. She had picked out the dress the month before, and fallen in love with it. It reminded her of the pink top Archie had told her he loved, and he wanted to see Archie wearing a pink bow tie.

Eden looked around the hall, her arms still wrapped around Archie's neck. She liked the atmosphere, it made her feel all warm and fuzzy inside.

'You look beautiful tonight, you know,' Archie whispered into her ear.

'You're just saying that,' Eden muttered.

'Hey,' Archie looked at her up and down, 'you're beautiful, you're gorgeous. I've never met anyone so stunning as you. I love you, I will never love anyone else. When you put yourself down, it puts me down. We're a pair, whatever hurts you hurts me, so please, don't hurt me.' Archie wrapped his arms back around her waist and she rested her head on his shoulder as they let the music play out.

'When tonight ends I want to tell you something, but you'll have to promise not to tell anyone else,' Archie spoke.

'Okay, you can trust me.' Eden looked up into his eyes and brushed her hand against his cheek.

'I know... I know I can.' He kissed her, and everything around them seemed like it froze in time. She wished they could freeze in time forever. But forever doesn't really last. The Back To School Dance was an annual thing that the school did every year, and it was always a success. Eden had just never taken a boy to it before, yet alone the love of her entire life. For the first time ever she had worn the ring he gave her. The disco lights surrounding them reflected off it and split into millions of tiny pieces on the walls. No one thought it was her though. Good.

Eden watched Archie walk up onto the stage where the DJ was. He was going to sing. Eden didn't know what, maybe a cover, or one of his songs she had heard before. But the music was different to anything she had heard before. Each note that followed was new. Well, it wasn't new, but the music was new. She hadn't heard this song. He had never performed it to her, yet alone anywhere else.

Archie looked distant up on the stage, but he was home. It was where he belonged. His hand moved up and down as it strummed against the guitar strings and he moved his head forward towards the microphone. She would either love it, or hate it. But she had never hated one of his songs. She could never hate one of his songs. Everyone around her had come together in their pairs, they looked deeply into eachothers eyes as he sang. She wanted to do the same, with Archie, but she couldn't. So she just stood there, and stared at him. Her eyes wandered every now and then, she wanted to see how everyone was reacting, but she could tell he was only looking at her, so she looked back up. He smiled as he sang, and she smiled back. The song was beautiful, and she wanted to cherish it forever.

When he finished he came straight back to Eden, who had rested at the back of the hall.

'Hey,' he said softly and took her hand. She didn't move, she just stayed there.

'That was beautiful, it was a beautiful song Arch.' She looked at him and smiled.

'I love you,' he kissed her forehead lightly and brought her into him. She held onto him and breathed in his smell.

'I love you too,' she replied, although she was pretty sure he didn't hear her.

'Now, come on, let's get out of here.' He took her hand and led her out of the hall and onto the streets. They walked, she didn't know where, but she liked it. The fresh breeze in her hair, on her face, on her sweaty palms. He looked even more handsome in the moonlight. Maybe the moonlight was his best look? They walked further, up the road and out of the town. The path ended and they were forced to go on the road, but they didn't care. She liked being reckless for one fleeting moment. The night was dark, but the air was warm, apart from a cool breeze. She held his hand tighter and looked up at him every once in a while. Sometimes just being silent was her favourite moment with him, because it's all they ever wanted the world to be.

'Eden there's something you need to know.' He stopped and faced her, they were still on the road, but there were no cars. It was safe.

'What?' She stroked his face and smiled.

'I've been asked to go to New York, to record an album. It won't take long, but they want me there for a month,' he said. His voice was shaking, like he was nervous. But he shouldn't be nervous.

'When are you going?' Eden asked. She didn't stop smiling.

'November, but I'll be back way before Christmas' he added. Eden thought she saw a tear emerge from his eye. She wiped it away gently.

'I'm proud of you, this is what you've always wanted.' He stopped shaking slightly and cupped her face in his hands.

'You're not angry?' He asked cautiously.

'Why would I be?' She brushed away the hair that had fallen in front of his eyes, 'I'm always going to love you. And this… this is just one step closer to everyone knowing your name.'

'And we'll Skype every day, that's a promise,' Archie spoke. His face was much closer to hers, she liked that feeling.

'And I'll visit, every weekend,' she added.

'You've just got to promise to send me all the work I miss,' he joked. She laughed, and so did he. Eden looked away, and then took his hand and they continued walking down the road, god knows where. She held his hand tight, he was all she wanted.

'You know it's been a year since I met you now,' Eden remarked.

'I couldn't have asked for a better year,' he squeezed her hand tighter.

And they continued walking up the road. Eden wished they could just keep on walking and not turn back. They were silent, they let the owls make their strange noises, and the few cars rush by.

'Eden whatever happens this year, you'll always be by my side, won't you?' He asked suddenly. Eden looked at him and smiled, she wrapped her arm around his so that they were walking arm in arm.

'I'm not going to leave your side. I don't think I can. You're too special to forget, you're worth too much to just disappear out of my life. I can't give you much, but I can give you my promise that I will never stop loving you.' She finished speaking, and it was silent. Even the nightly sounds stopped for a moment. It was like the earth was listening to them. Two people in love, two people afraid of what life would throw at them, and yet they trusted each other dearly. They didn't know how much the other person meant to them. They didn't know anything, and yet they knew everything.

She kissed him, and he kissed her, and suddenly they forgot about everything they had talked about, because they wanted to live in the moment. Moments are special, they're real time things. They're not the past, because you can't relive the past, they're not the future, because you can only dream of the future. In that moment they were stardust in dirt. Rainbows in showers of rain. They were infinite, never ending, eternal, preassigned. They were cosmic.

Every time she was out with Ezra she thought of Archie. It was like he had cemented himself into her head. She pulled away from Ezra and sat on her chair. He stood over her, and then sat down on his chair. She didn't speak, she looked around the restaurant, everyone seemed as if they hadn't even noticed they were dancing. Eden looked down at her feet, which tapped on the floor quietly. Her brain wanted to say something, but her mouth couldn't find the right words. Maybe she had made a mistake moving forward with Ezra. Maybe it wasn't the right time. What if Archie still loved her? She looked up at Ezra, who sat there on his phone, but clearly he was only looking at a blank screen.

'Tonight was great, thank you for taking me,' Eden smiled and pulled on her coat that hung from the back of her chair. He looked up from his phone and smiled back at her.

'Do you… do you want to come back to mine?' He stuttered. No, she didn't. She wanted to go home.

'I should probably get back home, Juliet's probably waiting for me.'

'Well, can I walk you?' He asked. No, she didn't want him to, but she said yes anyway.

'Yeah sure,' she nodded and followed him out of the restaurant.

New York was now dark and wet and loud. Ezra linked his arm through Eden's. It made her shudder, because that was what Archie did. She wanted to get home quickly, so she speed walked, and Ezra walked at her pace. She didn't say much, and neither did he.

When they got back to her apartment he kissed her goodbye and then walked away, and suddenly she was free again. Ezra was sweet, she really liked him, like really liked him, but she could never love him. And she was afraid that she was going to break his heart one day, but they would get to that when the time came.

Her bed was warm when she climbed in and pulled the covers up over her shoulders. She wanted to fall asleep quickly so that she could wake up and it was tomorrow. But you can't wish for the future, it comes when it's ready to come. Tomorrow wouldn't come until it was ready.

Seventeen

A week passed. Eden decided to ditch the *Here to Help* group. It wasn't helping her, and she didn't like it. Only Camille and Loren. She tried to remember the song Archie had played the night of the Back To School Dance, it was hard when you were trying not to look at the album or any part of him. But she gave up. It was the ninth song on the list, the second to last one. She traced fingers over the letters, writing it out so that maybe it would come to life and he would be there. *Love Song.*
It's funny, you'd think all of the songs on the album were love songs, and they were, in one way or another, but he named this one *Love Song*. Was it the most important love song? Eden thought that all of his songs were important, because she thought he could never love anything else more than her. Eden wanted to throw up, not because she was sick, but because she couldn't bare the thought of living a life not loving Archie. She didn't understand that you were allowed to fall in love more than once. You don't have to, but you're allowed. Because

people come and go, and that's how life happens. Eden wanted Archie to come, but come forever, and never go. And then he went, and she didn't know what to do. It was like they had finished their own novel, the character's stories ended, there was no more story to tell, no sequel. And so Archie opened a new book, complete with new characters and new adventures, and Eden opened one too. But Archie wasn't in her's, he never was. He was just a past story that had been closed.

She lay down on her bed, her arms wrapped tightly around the album and breathed in heavily. She wanted to remember everything. All of his freckles on his face, she wanted to connect all of them and see what pattern they created, a constellation maybe. She remembered when he thread his arms through hers and they lay on her bed talking endlessly into the night. She remembered when she would find him in the music room and they would sing and make music together. When his voice mashed with hers, or when his guitar strummed lightly to her playing the piano. The evenings they had together, lying by the side of the lake, or driving into the night, or walking up a road that led nowhere, and yet it led everywhere. She missed it all, The feeling of being loved by someone. The thought of having a life together after high school, having the freedom to spend every night together and not worrying about having to get home by eleven, because they already were home. She missed it all, and it hadn't even happened yet. She missed imagining what her future would be, because with him she saw a future.

Some people you can love so much, but you have to remember that you will never love someone as much as you will miss them.

Eden decided to take a walk, she wanted to walk like she used to walk with Archie, because it made her happy. The sun decided to make an appearance, but it was still cold enough to have to wear a jacket. So she wore her grey one that made her feel warm and cosy and all the feelings you should feel when you feel warm. She wanted to go to the park, and walk around it, and then come home. She hadn't walked through a park in a long time, she wasn't sure what to expect. A few trees? Little kids playing on the swings? Dogs running around out of control?

Her phone buzzed in her coat pocket. It was Juliet.

Invite Ezra over tonight, Jason's coming too. We can have a double date kind of evening.

Of course she wanted to have Ezra over, just to take her mind off of things, that's what he was there for, he just didn't know it.

Will do. What are you planning?

She kept looking up from her phone to see where she was walking.

We could get a chinese takeaway, maybe play a game of some sort. Jason's got loads, I can ask him to bring some with him :)

She used to play board games with Archie. Scrabble was their favourite, because they liked coming up with crazy words to place on the board.

Just don't request Scrabble. I can't face playing that game.

She sent it without realising, and it was out in the world. Eden stuffed her phone in her pocket and carried on walking. Maybe if she walked far enough she could leave everything behind. She felt her phone buzz in her pocket, Juliet had replied, but she didn't want to answer it. She didn't even want to look at it.

Across the park she could see a gate to leave, her feet walked faster as she headed for it, they could barely keep up with her. And then she stopped. Because she saw something. Strung up on the railings was a poster, or Archie, except he wasn't Archie. He was Archer King. Eden walked slowly to it and stared at it. His hair looked wet and curly, like he had just been playing on stage and was now drenched in sweat. He had dark eyes and even darker pupils. She knelt down so that it was at eye level. Eden wanted to reach out and touch it, but she was in public. That would just be weird. He was dressed in all black and had a guitar, an electric guitar, hanging across his shoulders. Archie never played the electric guitar. Not with Eden at least. Suddenly Eden was overheating and sweat poured down her face. It was indistinguishable from her tears which fell from her eyes. And she was finally-finally crying in public.

Eden didn't know how long she sat there looking up at the poster, but she knew someone was behind her after a while.

'Eden,' a voice said behind her. Eden turned around sharply, Camille had squatted behind her, and she looked stunning.

'I'm... I'm sorry,' she tried to wipe away the tears, but it was too late.

'Do you want to talk?' Camille held out her hand and brought Eden to her feet. There was dirt on the back of her jeans which she brushed off. Camille's children were running around behind them, they looked like they were having fun. Four of them. Two girls, two boys, and all of them looked happy. How could a seven year old have more happiness than Eden, they hadn't even lived a decade yet and somehow they were overcome with joy and happiness.

Eden nodded and wiped away more of her tears.

'Okay, let me just send the kids off.' She called her children over, they were well behaved and came immediately.

'This is mummy's friend, we're just going to have a little chat. Here is some money, go and buy yourself an icecream and play on the swings for a while,' she handed over a 10 dollar bill to what looked like the oldest, a boy, maybe eight or nine years old. He had dark hair like Camille's and his smile was gorgeous.

The children ran off to the play park, Camille watched them until they were safe by the swings.

'Here, we can go and sit over there.' Camille led Eden to a bench by the path, it was slightly wet, but she sat on her coat.

'You don't have to tell me, if you don't want to, but why were you sitting in front of a poster of Archer King?' Camille asked. Eden sat there, she could tell the truth, or lie, again. It seemed like the easiest option, but now it was different. He was everywhere, apart from her life. She took a deep breath.

'I was just... his music I relate to, a lot,' Eden lied. She looked down at her feet and then back up at Camille, who was smiling. She so desperately wanted to tell the truth, but the truth can be ugly sometimes.

'And it reminded you of a past relationship?' Camile questioned.

'Yeah,' she nodded. Eden dug her fingernails into the palms of her hands. It was a frequent thing she had been doing recently. Crescent moons appeared where they dug deeper. Scars, but she could hide them.

'Look at those kids over there,' Camille pointed to her four children who were swinging from the frame, sliding down the slide and climbing up the poles. 'They remind me constantly every day of their father, Mason, the oldest, he looks just like his dad. But I moved on, and I see the good they have. Now I'm not saying stop listening to the music, because if it makes you feel better, then I don't want to stop you. I stopped thinking about their dad, and started thinking about them, who they were, what great things they will do in their life. Maybe you should start thinking about what you're going to do instead of reminiscing over the past. That's not going to heal you, your dreams will. You have to have a goal, otherwise you'll just keep falling back off the board and you won't be able to climb back up.'

Eden nodded, again. It seemed as though it was a common occurrence for her to just nod when she didn't know what to say.

'I'm sorry I didn't come to the meeting this morning. I just feel like I don't fit in there, everyone has diagnosed mental health issues, and I'm just, well… me. I'm so obsessed over this relationship I've had, and that's not normal. I can't put one foot in front of the other without thinking about him, or where he is, or what he's doing. Everyone there talks about how they've overcome depression, or how they cope with it. I'm not coping, I'm just living. I wake up every day and I don't know whether I'll be happy or sad, or both. I don't live to fulfil life any more, I just live so that one day I'll be gone. That's all I want.' Eden stopped speaking, she felt like she had said too much. She felt like she was living life just to get through it so that one day her story would just be tied up in a little bow and thrown off the edge of a cliff.

'Eden have you ever heard of something called bipolar disorder? It's a mental health condition that can affect your mood, from one extreme to the other. Some people call it manic depression, it runs in families, but it can be treated. Its episodes consist of days when you feel low and lethargic, this is the depressive side of it, and then there are episodes where you feel very high and over active,' Camille explained. For the first time, Eden actually listened willingly.

'But I don't feel high and over active, ever,' she stated. Camille looked over at her children, and then back at Eden.

'During the mania phase you may feel very happy, or have lots of ideas in your head that you think you can achieve,' Camille continued saying.

Ezra. She thought she could achieve happiness through Ezra.

'There's also moments where you might experience psychosis, where you see things, or hear things that aren't actually there. Or become convinced about things that aren't true,' Camille added.

The shower. Last week she had a shower and was convinced that Archie was there with her. She believed that she and Archie were meant for eachother, that they were cosmic. Was this all just part of the psychosis that comes with bipolar?

'What... What causes bipolar disorder?' Eden asked. Her voice was quiet, and she was scared.

'The exact cause is unknown, no one really knows, but there are a number of things that can trigger an episode.'

'What? Like what?' Eden asked again.

'Extreme stress, overwhelming problems, life changing events, or just genetic and chemical factors.'

Bingo. Everything started to fall into place, slowly, but it fell.

'Eden from what you've told me, I think it's clear that you're hurt, and lost, and you need someone to talk to, about this.'

Well duh, that's like the whole point.

'How... How do I go about doing that?' Eden tucked her hair behind her ears and looked up at Camille.

'Well, I can recommend a psychiatrist who will talk to you, and help you get the help you need,' Camille said.

Eden nodded, again. Camille's children came running up to them, the youngest jumped on Camille's lap and the other three hung around them.

'I'll text you,' Camille smiled, and then she was off with her children. Four little people that shaped her into who she was today.

Eden walked slowly home. She still hadn't read the message Juliet had sent her, she didn't really care what it said. There was another poster of Archie on a wall, and another one that was stuck onto the side of a bus. Eden tried to ignore them, but she couldn't. He was there, watching over her. And she wanted him more than anything, and yet she couldn't have him.

The streets were busy for a Thursday afternoon, she weaved herself in and out of the crowd of people that hustled and bustled. Shit. She hadn't texted Ezra. Opening her phone she saw the unread message Juliet had sent her.

Jason's bringing Monopoly. Get ready, it's going to be a long night :)

Why had she been so afraid to read that message? It had nothing to do with Scrabble, or Archie, or Ezra for that matter.

She sent Ezra a message telling him to come over later, he said yes, she was happy.

Eighteen

They were all over each other. Juliet and Jason. Hugging and squeezing and kissing, it made Eden feel sick to her stomach. She and Ezra just sat back in the corner, and acted normally. They hadn't even ordered food yet, clearly they were busy doing other things. Eden couldn't even look over at them, so she just looked at Ezra, his sweet curly hair looked extra curly today. He was wearing a flannel shirt, it made him kind of look like a farmer, but it strangely suited him.
'How long have they been together?' Ezra whispered into her ear. They were sitting on her bed in the corner of the living room playing some form of card game.
'Just over a month, but they act like a married couple,' she replied. Eden looked over her shoulder at them again, they had been lying on the sofa. It was disgusting.
'Well, I'm hungry,' Ezra exclaimed, 'hey guys!' He called over to Juliet and Jason. They sat up and looked over.
'Wanna get food?'

Eden noticed them roll their eyes, but she didn't say anything. Instead, they just nodded and the four of them sat together around the coffee table to order. Eden wasn't hungry, she didn't want to eat anything, but she knew Juliet would say something.

When their food arrived Juliet sat on Jason's lap and kept looking back at him, smiling and feeding each other food like they were babies. Eden could tell Ezra wanted her to do the same thing, he looked up every now and again from his food, smiled at Eden, and then went back to eating. She felt bad, like he was being left out. Juliet was right, it would be a long night. A long night of looking at Juliet and Jason make out on the sofa in front of them and be all affectionate to each other. This time, Eden rolled her eyes and turned to face Ezra.

'Are you okay?' She asked him. He looked up and stared into her eyes. His eyes looked brighter than usual, maybe she had just never looked at them this way before.

'Yeah I'm fine. I'm just tired,' he sighed.

'You can go if you want, you don't have to stay.' Eden rubbed his hand and sighed too.

'Do you mind?' He asked.

'No, it's fine. If anything, I might go out and clear my head,' she spoke, 'but I'll walk you home, if that's okay?' He nodded, and they stood up. Eden pulled her jacket over her shoulders and slipped on her black boots. Ezra went to the bathroom quickly, and Juliet and Jason were too busy with each other to realise what they were doing. Eden grabbed her bag, but not her small bag. This one was larger, and had more space in it. She stuffed in a few

pairs of clothes and Archie's album, and then proceeded to pile in her phone charger and the pebble Archie had given her that night at the lake. The pink top went in last, Archie's favourite pink top.
Ezra came out of the bathroom and put his jacket on too, and then his shoes, and then they were gone. They walked down the stairs to the street, the air was cool, but it wasn't raining. That was a first. Eden held his hand, for the first time, as they walked to his apartment.
She wanted to say something, anything, but she couldn't. She didn't know what to say, he was so innocent and gentle, she didn't want to hurt his feelings. Ezra was like this delicate butterfly that you couldn't damage. He was mysterious, she knew nothing about him, and part of her didn't want to know anything. Because if she knew too much, she could fall in love. And Eden didn't think she could ever fall in love again.
They turned the corner, and then another corner, people were still out on the streets, when were they not? Eden linked her arm through his and rested her head on his shoulder as they walked.
'You can stay, you know? At mine, if you want to give the JJ's some space,' Ezra asked.
'The JJ's? Now that is a new name for them,' she laughed. 'It sounds like some drug you take when you're sixteen.'
'What type of place did you come from? Because the only drugs I knew about were paracetamol and cannabis,' he exclaimed.

'You came from practically royalty. You didn't grow up in a town where in your school there was a club dedicated to the drug dealers,' Eden admitted.
'True, but it doesn't mean I want to be royalty.' Ezra continued walking, and Eden followed.
'What do you mean?' She clung onto his arm and looked up at him.
'Being told what to do, where to go, what not to do, it gets kind of annoying after a while. I was never given freedom, until now. So basically now I'm living out my childhood, whilst in my twenties.'
Eden was quiet, she thought a while, she thought long and hard. That explained his bedroom, and why it looked like a teenage boys den.
'Well, I was going to catch a train up to Iowa now, and leave for a while, but you could come with me, if you wanted to,' she asked. He didn't reply immediately. Maybe she was making a mistake herself?
'You're trying to make me run away with you huh?' He joked. True, but technically she wasn't running away. She was just going home.
'Its stupid I know, I shouldn't have asked.' Eden turned her head away and released her grip from his arm. It started raining.
'No, it's not stupid. I just, I don't know who you are, you've told me nothing about you. How am I supposed to go half away across the country and not even know your middle name?'
'Delilah.' She turned her head sharply to look at him as they walked.

'Okay but that's not enough. Like who are you? Why is it that whenever I see you you're always crying? Why are you so obsessed with sad songs?' He vented. He really went there.
'I want to tell you, but the truth is, I don't know. I don't know why I always cry, and I like sad songs because they're the songs with the most emotion in,' Eden answered. She saw that he took a gulp.
'I'll come with you, if you promise me to tell me about you,' he said.
'I can't promise you anything,' she was crying as she replied. Again with the crying, why did that always happen?
'Then promise me you won't cry.' He wiped away her tears. She nodded. She wanted to kiss him, something inside of her made her feel found, she wasn't found, but he was like a lighthouse in her darkness. Eden wanted to believe he could save her, but it was only a matter of time. She wanted to kiss him even more, to make sure he was the right way forward. To make sure she was making the right decision. She cupped his face in her hands like she did with Archie, he looked even more like Archie tonight. Eden kissed him like she kissed Archie, gently, and passionately. This wasn't a mistake. Not yet. Her hands were cold and shaking, he took them and blew on them before rubbing them between his.
'Come on,' he took her hand again and they walked to his apartment. The steps were steep and slippery as she carefully climbed them, her backpack bounced up and

down on her back. Eden's phone buzzed, she knew it would be Juliet, but she didn't answer it.
She stepped back into his teenage boy like bedroom. Something about it made her want to strip back her walls and have her dream room from when she was fourteen again. Even his bag reminded her of the boys that walked the corridors freshman year of highschool.
'You know when we get there, you can stay in the spare bedroom in our house. You don't have to get a hotel or anything, not that there are any hotels there,' she said sarcastically.
'Do your parents even know you're coming?' He asked.
'No, but I thought I'd surprise them,' she stated.
'Yeah, with me,' Ezra swung his bag onto his back, 'when's the train?'
Crap. She hadn't even got train tickets. She didn't even know if there were trains running to Iowa. Surely there would be, they go everywhere.
'I'll check now.' She pulled out her phone and saw Juliet's messages. All five of them.
Eden where are you? And where's Ezra?
And another one:
Eden we're going to start the game without you.
Followed by another one:
Call me, please. Where did you go?
Then another one:
This isn't funny where are you?
And then one more:
Where the fuck are you Eden? You're starting to scare me.

Eden felt kind of bad, and then not. So she ignored them and tried to find a train that would send her and Ezra to Iowa.

The two of them sat on the floor of the train station eating cookies and drinking coffee. It had just gone nine at night, the station was almost empty.

'When's the train arriving?' Ezra asked and stuffed another cookie into his mouth. Eden looked behind her at the table of arriving trains. She glared at it, the bright orange lights glared back at her like they were having a staring contest.

'Ten minutes, hopefully.' She smiled at him, and he smiled back.

'What are you even going to do there? It's not like Iowa is full of exciting things,' he laughed.

'See my mum, my dad, maybe visit some of my favourite places. I haven't been there in a long time,' she added.

'I've never been to Iowa, full disclosure.'

'Not many people have to be honest.'

They got on the train, and it pulled away quickly. The journey would be long, but it wasn't the first time she had made the journey.

That night they talked a lot, about themselves, about each other, about everything. And yet Eden managed not to mention anything about herself (that was true). She wanted to look out of the windows and scan the landscape as they moved out of New York and into the wider world, but the night had dawned and all she could see was black. Eden just wanted to lock away her brain for a little while so she didn't have to think about Archie, she wanted to

enjoy spending time with Ezra. Someone who actually wanted her. She realised Ezra was this incredibly strong magnet that she was drawn to, even if she didn't want to be. And he was attractive (no pun intended). No matter how hard she tried, Ezra was there, ready to be a shoulder to cry on, even if she had promised not to cry, and even more so he didn't know why she cried. But he was there. He was soft, and caring, and wanted to spend time with her. Her heart felt wanted when she was near him, and yet she didn't want him the way he wanted her. He was falling in love, she was trying to fall out of love.
'Do you know, *Love of My Life?* By Queen?' He asked as they finished playing yet another card game. She lost, but she had the queen of hearts in her hand, so she deep down thought that was a winner.
'I love it,' she muttered and shuffled the cards to play again. Her legs were crossed on the uncomfortable train seat and she had managed to find a blanket that the train servers were handing out, like they do on a plane.
'Here,' he handed her a headphone, and he took the other, and they listened to the song. She didn't look at him when it played, she just listened, like she always did. The song reminded her of her and Archie. A strong but broken relationship. The love of her life.
Eden shuffled the cards in her hand without even realising. And then she dropped them. They spread across the floor under her seat. The headphone fell out of her ear when she bent down to pick them up. She collected them in her hands and brought her head back up, she was crying, but Ezra wasn't allowed to see. Eden

put the headphone back in her ear, the song was finishing, she listened again.

'You hear about how couples have a song, that they like to listen to together over and over again. I always thought it was *Songbird,* for us. But when I listened to this one, it spoke clearer. I don't know why, but I wanted to have a song, together,' he explained.

Eden thought it was cute, but he referred to them as a couple. Were they a couple? Or just a couple of people who find comfort when they're around each other?

'It's perfect.' She remembered saying that to Archie all the time when he played her a song. Ezra would never sing to her, not like Archie did. She wasn't even sure if he sang to begin with.

Eden dealt out the cards one last time and they played. It was a distraction, from everything and everyone. Ezra won, again. But Eden still had the queen of hearts in her hands. Maybe it was a sign. But for what?

Her phone buzzed and Juliet's name appeared.

Eden if you don't reply I'm calling the police. Where are you?

Maybe calling the police wasn't such a bad idea. It would keep people occupied. But she didn't want the attention.

I'm with Ezra, on a train, going up to Iowa for a bit. I'll see you soon x

She sent the message and then buried her phone deep in her bag and fell asleep. When she woke the sky was brighter and bluer and the fields were covered in dirt. Home, at last.

Eden wasn't sure whether to regret bringing Ezra with her. She was worried she would leave him out, or forget about him, or both. She looked at him whilst he slept, his eyes were glued shut and his hair had flopped over his forehead.

And she thought things could be a lot worse, because she could be going up there alone, and then there would be no one to tell the story of how she tried to bring her rebound home to relive all of her memories she had with her ex, with him. Or that when they kissed on the side of the lake all she saw was Archie staring back at her. Or when they sat in the middle of a clearing, surrounded by trees, he didn't play a song to her, because he didn't know how to write one. He was a music nerd, hopeless romantic that wanted a slo-mo, heart palpitating kind of romance, and she couldn't give it to him. Because she didn't know how.

Nineteen

It was just as she had left it. Her bedroom was small and simplistic. The walls were covered in pink wallpaper and had fairy lights hanging from the ceiling. The bed was made, with pink and gold pillows placed neatly on top. Dust had collected on the mirror, her dressing table, and the window ledges where pictures of her and Archie were still placed.
Shit. Fuck. Crap. Ezra was going to walk in any minute now and recognise Archie from, well everywhere. She scooped up any remaining photo there was of them and pushed them under her bed. Clearly her mother hadn't spent any time clearing out any last trace of him, maybe she was just as obsessed as Eden was.
Ezra wandered in, looking up at the ceiling, at the floor and then at the walls.
'This is a nice room you got,' he exclaimed. It was true, she had been blessed with the best room in the house in her opinion.
'Thanks. My mum still hasn't got round to clearing anything out,' she laughed. There were old trophies lined

up from various karate competitions she had won when she was twelve. Ezra picked one up and laughed.
'You did karate?' He asked. Eden pretended to throw a karate move.
'Still do,' she almost kicked him, 'well, at least I still can. Haven't had lessons in years.' Fact. She hadn't had lessons since before she met Archie.
'This is basically what my room looked like when I was thirteen, it hasn't really changed,' she admitted.
'So you're telling me that I'm walking into thirteen year old Eden's bedroom?' He joked.
She nodded and laughed.
'I've never felt more blessed.' Ezra sat on her bed and looked around again.
'It's pretty embarrassing if you ask me. I wish my mum cleaned it out after the… after I moved to New York,' she stopped and then rephrased what she was going to say. It almost slipped out. After the break up. He didn't know about a break up. She couldn't tell him anything.
Eden heard movement downstairs. Her parents had arrived, and she still hadn't told them she was coming. She ran down the stairs, but slowly. Can you even run down the stairs slowly?
'Mum!' She shouted as she came into view of her parents.
'Eden!' Her mum threw open her arms and Eden ran towards her, hugging her and breathing in her fresh lavender smell. 'What are you doing here?' She asked as she looked Eden up and down and then in the eye.

'All honesty, not really sure, but I missed you,' she hugged her mum again, and then hugged her dad who was standing behind Mrs Harper.
'Why didn't you call? Or tell me you were coming,' her mum questioned. Eden stood in front of her parents, gulped, sighed, and then showed a weak smile.
'Well, last time I called you, you shut me down, remember?'
Her mum stared at the floor. The floorboards were old and needed replacing.
'That was a different time. But you're here now, that's what matters.' Mrs Harper hugged Eden again, and again. Ezra slowly descended the stairs, Eden turned around and smiled, before beckoning him to join them.
'Mum, this is my… friend, Ezra. He came with me,' Eden said.
'Ezra, nice to meet you. Welcome.' Mrs Harper shook his hand and studied him. Eden didn't like it when she did that, but it was a character trait she had.
'Thank you for having me, I know it's short notice,' he said shyly.
'No don't be silly. I love having visitors.' It was true. Mrs Harper was known to have big gatherings frequently in her house. She was the town's mother as they called her.
'Okay, well we're gonna go upstairs,' Eden started walking up the stairs.
'Wait don't you want to talk a while? I haven't seen you in ages,' her mum called out after her. There was a reason Eden hadn't gone to see her any time soon. For this exact reason.

'I'm just gonna go upstairs for a bit, if you don't mind, to get settled in.' She smiled and looked back at Ezra who was leaning on the side of the staircase.

'I'll call you down for dinner then,' Mrs Harper kissed Eden's cheek and smiled ecstatically, 'it's good to have you back Eden.'

Eden smiled and went back up stairs. Ezra followed, she could hear his footsteps behind her. Her window curtains were shut tight, when she opened them a wave of dust splashed in her face and made her cough and wheeze.

'So when you said my mother was royalty, you forgot about your own basically,' Ezra commented.

'No, your mother is more *I want to be Queen one day.* My mother is a *If I'm not president I'll die,* type of person. She likes being in charge.'

'I can tell,' he exclaimed.

Eden jumped onto her bed and kicked off her shoes. They landed just under her dressing table. Ezra did the same and they lay looking up to the ceiling, surrounded by Eden's miscellaneous pillows that she got when she was thirteen.

'Why haven't you been back in so long?' He asked. Eden didn't want to answer, because she could tell the truth, or lie again. She lied. No surprise there.

'I was so happy in New York,' she started. False, she was miserable in New York and tried to kill herself. 'I just didn't want to leave and come up here where nothing really happens.' False again. Everything that she enjoyed happened here. Archie was here. And yet he wasn't.

Eden took a deep breath in, and somehow it smelt like Archie. His scent lingered on the bed sheets, on the walls and in the carpet. He lingered everywhere. Eden desperately wanted to look at the pictures she had thrown under her bed. She wanted to remember those moments. The ones she had framed. Her heart was racing as she tried to rack her memory of the photos that were under her bed. What photos had she framed? Eden wanted to reach down and look at them. She wanted it more than anything in the entire world. But now that Ezra was with her, there wouldn't be a single minute when she would be able to do that. She looked over at him. He held his phone just above his head and was looking through some form of social media platform. He was breathing heavily, Eden wanted to shut him up, but she couldn't.
Her head was heavy, and she just wanted to fall asleep, but her phone buzzed, again. And she could already tell who it was going to be.
I don't understand why you left so suddenly. Why didn't you tell me, or say goodbye, or just stay in general? Eden I'm your best friend, I deserve to know what's going on right? Just, promise me you'll come back soon. -J
Eden held the phone close to her chest and closed her eyes. She tried to plan out what she was going to say back.
'Where's the bathroom?' Ezra asked suddenly. He sat up and stretched out his arms and legs, before standing up. 'Just across the hallway to the left,' she smiled. Eden watched him walk out of the room and then quickly fell to

the floor and pulled out a few of the photo frames. Eden's eighteenth birthday. She was wearing a dark purple dress and golden heels so that she was almost Archie's height. Her smile was the happiest smile she had ever seen.

Eden didn't want a big eighteenth birthday party like everyone else did. She wanted it to be small, she didn't even want a birthday party to begin with, but Juliet insisted. She said it was this tradition that everyone that went to their highschool had to have a party of some sort. Fuck traditions. But she had one anyway. Just her and a handful of other people. Her birthday was so close to Christmas she could call it a Christmas party, but mixing the two together was a bad idea.

She went down to her basement, Juliet was already there laying out decorations, blowing up balloons and organising the food. Archie sat there in the corner on his guitar.

'Hey,' she said as she walked down the stairs and into the basement. It always had this stench from drains, but she just sprayed gallons of perfume and usually it was fine.

'Oh my gosh Eden you look stunning!' Juliet exclaimed and stopped what she was doing to run up to her and give her a hug. Her purple dress fell just above her knees and stuck to her body like glue. It showed off her slim figure and lean legs. Eden looked behind Juliet, Archie was smiling at her, like he had just been shown the most beautiful thing in the world.

'You look amazing.' He stood up and walked over to her, kissing her freshly coloured lips, smudging them slightly.

'What's the time?' Eden looked around for a clock.
'Almost seven, people will be here soon,' Archie replied.
'Okay, well is everything ready?' Eden looked around the room again at the balloons and banners that hung from the walls. It was the cringiest, most embarrassing decorated room she had ever seen, but Juliet and Archie had tried too hard to make it perfect.
More people turned up than expected. The word had clearly got around. Eden stayed by the walls as more and more people walked down the stairs and jumped up and down to the music. The basement was getting too crowded and she was worried people would migrate to the upstairs area.
She sat down on a chair next to the food and ate. Probably too much, but that didn't really matter at the time. There were people she didn't even know in her house. She tried to make out who had actually turned up, but they were moving too fast for her to properly catch a glimpse of their face.
Tyler Kramer (played football and had probably had sex with most of the girls in their class), Martha Mules (who was the bitch), Willow Jones (the bitch's sidekick), Sean Rutherford (bad guy who rode a motorcycle to school everyday), Nellie Foster (Eden was friends with her in sixth grade, and now they weren't), Callum Brown (why was he even in her house), and plenty more that Eden could barely recognise under the dark lighting and/or the amount of makeup they were wearing.
Archie came up and kissed her, he had been with some of his friends that actually were invited. He was slightly drunk

and tipsy, his breath smelt of alcohol, but Eden found that somewhat sexy. His hair was slightly wet from sweat, or he had been drowned in some form of liquidy substance, alcohol most likely.

He kissed her even more, she grew more and more accepting of that fact that he reeked of alcohol. As long as he wasn't doing drugs, Eden was cool with that. They were teenagers, what was the harm in taking a sip of alcohol every once in a while?

'Do you want to sneak out?' She heard him say as they made out. She nodded as she kissed him back and clung to his neck. It was sweating too, her hands slid down it like a waterslide and fell down his back.

Eden didn't manage to get away that easily. She was the host after all. Her excuse was that she needed to go talk to her mum, Juliet was suspicious and said she'd hold fort down in the basement. Archie followed her up the stairs to her bedroom and shut the door behind him. He wobbled as he walked towards her and took off the top he was wearing.

'You look… incredibly hot tonight,' he whispered into her ear. He brushed his hand across her thigh and picked her up, kissing her. She felt hot and sticky, like Archie had passed on all of his sweatiness to her. She slipped off her dress and let Archie make kisses in the well of her neck.

'You're drunk, you know that,' she said. He propped himself up on his elbows and looked down at her.

'I love you,' he slurred.

'Yes I know that, but you're drunk, and you don't know what you're doing,' she stopped him.

'I love you,' he said again, but the words merged into one as he said it. His breath was warm and full of energy.
'Archie wait a minute.'
He kissed her like he was hungry, running his hands up her thighs across her hips and around her waist. She loved it, but it wasn't right. Drunk Archie wasn't a pretty sight.
'Archie can we talk,' she asked as she let him kiss her body. He sat up, his body half on top of hers, he looked worried.
'Yeah sure, what about?' He ran his fingers softly across her chest and down her stomach. She smiled and giggled a bit.
'Can we… maybe wait until later? Until everyone's gone?' Her head buried deeper into the soft pillow she was lying on. He nodded and stood up from the bed and but his top back on. Eden pulled her dress over her head and Archie zipped up the back, he wobbled from the alcohol, but he kept his balance.
As they descended the stairs to the basement there was an embarrassing cheer, the music had stopped and everyone was making noises you'd hear at a football game.
'Looks like the lovebirds have finally finished!' She heard someone say.
'Did you miss us?' Someone else cooed.
'I fucking knew they were off banging somewhere!' Somebody shouted. Eden rolled her eyes at that one.

'Right, no more alcohol,' she whispered into Archie's ear. She was confused as to how the alcohol even got into her house, she hadn't provided any.

The room grew loud with chatter and people finally dispersed into the cold December night. What was left of the basement was not for the faint hearted. Empty cans of various drinks, some Eden had never heard of, and some people had snuck into the house. The food was emptied across the floor, and balloons were scattered. Eden looked around at everything and sat on the floor. Juliet joined her, sitting with her and crossing her legs.

'Did you make out with anyone?' Eden joked. Juliet gave her a harsh stare and then laughed.

'Sean Rutherford. He's a surprisingly good kisser you know,' she exclaimed, smiling and shrugging her shoulders.

'You never know. Maybe bad boy Sean is the one?' Eden said sarcastically.

'Just because I kiss someone doesn't automatically put me in a relationship with them,' Juliet lectured.

'Well, it's just one extra boy to add to your list of kissed but not dated.'

Archie came down the stairs, slowly, he held onto the bannister tightly. Juliet stood up when he saw him.

'I'll let you two be, I'll see you on Monday,' Juliet tapped Eden's head and headed up the stairs as Archie came down.

Eden rocked back and forth where she was sitting, she let Archie come to her and sit down. He had dark circles under his eyes and was sweating heavily. He wasn't a hyper drunk, he was more of an emotional wreck drunk. Eden found those people more attractive anyway. He crossed his legs and sat in front of her, cute and adorable as always.

'I'm sorry,' he announced.

'For what?'

'For being a dick.'

'You weren't a dick. You were just excited,' she moved closer to him and ran her fingers through his hair. It was knotted and matted and felt disgusting.

'Happy Birthday by the way.' He showed her the time on his phone, it was gone midnight, which meant it was now her birthday. The two of them just needed to sleep, they looked awful.

'Give me that,' Eden reached out for his phone and opened the camera. She pulled him down so that they were lying on the floor next to each other and held the phone in front. Eden wasn't sure how many photos she took of them that night, they were just being silly and in love. They were characters out of a movie. They were thoroughly alive and they were adorably beautiful.

Eden heard Ezra walking back down the corridor to her room. She took one final look at the photo, they looked tired, and happy. She pushed the photo frames under the bed, and then pulled the one of her in the purple dress back out and stuffed it into her already full backpack. That one was staying with her.

Ezra came back in, and then soon they were called down to dinner. Her mother's spaghetti bolognese was the best she had ever had, ever since she was little she had always loved it. But this time it reminded her of the scene in Lady and the Tramp. About love, and how she was torn between two people, one that she loved that didn't love her back, and one that loved her but she didn't love back. And although Ezra hadn't specifically said 'I love you', Eden knew it was coming. And when it did, she knew it would hit her like a tidal wave and she wouldn't survive.

Twenty

Eden knew what she had to do. Well, she didn't have to do it, she wanted to do it, she needed to do it. And having Ezra there only eased the pain slightly. But he was there, and that made her happy. She wasn't sure how it would make her feel, going everywhere she had been with Archie. Would there be a border blocking her from going in and making the same mistakes again? If this was the only way to fall in love, then he would take it. And maybe in the process she'd fall out of love with Archie.
'So, what have you got planned today?' Her mum asked as they sat down eating breakfast. The kitchen smelled of burnt coffee, her dad was known to be an awful cook, or person to be in the kitchen in general. That's why her mum did everything.
'Probably look around town, show Ezra some of the sights, not that there are many,' she added. Her hair was the neatest it had been that year, freshly brushed and straightened, and the shampoo she had used wasn't just a cheap one she had found in a corner store and was

probably for men anyway. It was expensive shampoo, her mother's favourite.

'Okay, well you guys have fun, I'm going to head out for work soon.' She smiled and stood up from the table, bringing her empty bowl and mug with her. Her parents were both dentists, they met at dentists school or whatever you call it. She always thought it was cute how they loved each other and their job. And that they were passionate about it. She was jealous of their love story, because it was real, and it lasted.

Eden finished her breakfast quickly, she could see Ezra had already finished and was waiting patiently for her. At least he had manners.

By the time they had left the house and locked up it was almost eleven. She wanted to take Ezra to the highschool. That was where she fell in love with Archie, maybe she could fall in love with Ezra there too. She remembered the walk easily, like she had only done it yesterday. Archie used to walk with her every morning, he would knock on her door and wait until she came out and then they'd walk hand in hand. Most of the time turning up fashionably late, but somehow the teachers never cared.

Eden took Ezra's hand as they walked, she wanted to see if it would work. His hand was soft and the rings on his fingers dug into her knuckles. She hadn't realised he wore rings. There were lots of them, silver ones with celtic symbols, bejeweled ones, and this one that had a dragon on. That one was her favourite.

He just followed wherever he took her, it was perfect. She could lead him right into a volcano and he would go. He trusted her strangely.
When she stepped into the school she was overcome with nostalgia and memories from last year. She could see herself walking down the corridor with Archie, or Juliet, or both of them.
'So, this is where you went to school,' Ezra exclaimed as he looked up at the high ceilings and across at the courtyard.
'Yeah, this is where the magic happened.' She led him through the corridors and stopped outside a door. The music room. When she opened the door a cold draft hit her. No one used this room anymore. It really was her and Archie's safe space. Eden rubbed her arms, it was cold. No, it was freezing. Like she had just walked into a freezer or something like it. The piano had a thin layer of dust over it, she blew at it, but all that came back was a thick face of dust that got into her eyes. Ezra turned the light on and the room partly came to life.
'What happened here?' He asked as he walked over to Eden who had sat down at the piano stool.
'This is where I came to play, I guess no one has been in here this year,' She opened the piano lid and brushed her fingers across the keys like she used to do last year. It would probably be out of tune, but that never really bothered her.
'Are you going to play?' He sat next to her on the stool. She shrugged her shoulders and looked at him.

'I don't know what to play.' False, she wanted to play the first song Archie ever played to her in that room. *The Brightest.* Maybe if she played it then she would fall in love with Ezra, because that's what happened the last time.

She pressed her fingers down on the keys and at last they created a sound. Mellow and raw. She liked it. One note came after the other and it was all coming back to her again. The key turned major to minor to major again. She knew Ezra was a soft rabbit and that if he found out about anything she was doing he would hop right off the earth. She didn't want to hurt him, ever.

When she played she could see Archie standing there, watching over her like an archangel, making sure she didn't play a wrong note. But he wasn't there, it was just the hallucinations she had. That song was the first song he wrote for her, she wanted to treasure it forever.

'It's a pretty song,' he commented and she finished playing and moved her fingers from the keys.

'I've always liked it, ever since it came out.' Eden turned her head so that she was looking at him in the eyes. They were shining, like the brightest stars. Eden pressed her lips against his, she wanted to just get lost in the moment. To forget all the ugly in her life, just for one moment, and ask for redemption. She wanted to fleet all of the thrills and glory of her life, start over brand new. Eden thought that kissing Ezra then would change everything. She thought that playing that song and then kissing him would make her fall in love. But it didn't change a thing. She was still just as lost as she was before, more so now. She

brought her fingers up to her lips, was there a problem with her?
'That was... nice,' he spoke as he continued to look into her eyes. She looked away quickly.
'You're welcome.'
It hadn't worked. She loved Archie more than ever, and yet here was Ezra, and she felt bad for him. He wasn't a prop in this game of get your fiance back, or switch fiances, or just a prop in her game.
She moved from sitting on the stool to sitting on the floor by the bookcase filled with records and old music books. Ezra crossed his legs as he sat down next to her.
'Why did you bring me here?' He asked. He wasn't smiling. He was serious.
She sighed, she couldn't tell him the truth, the truth would break him.
'It wasn't so much you. I just wanted to see what they had done with the place,' she replied. Eden had brought her knees up to her chest and was rocking back and forth.
'And what did you discover?'
'Nothing. Absolutely nothing.' Eden rocked back and forth again, she was cold, and there was no heating. The posters she and Archie had stuck up on the walls still hung there, although some of them draped and looked like they just wanted to be ripped off and thrown in the bin. Eden felt like that too.
'You know at my highschool they had a music room too, but no one ever used it. I sometimes went in, and tried to teach myself piano, but I never got anywhere with it,' Ezra started saying, 'clearly I wasn't made for the spotlight.'

Eden laughed and smiled for the first time that day.
'Yeah I wanted to be a singer, I still do, kind of. But I don't think it's the right career for me,' she admitted.
'Why not?' Ezra tilted his head as he said it.
'I don't want to be famous anymore.' She sighed and began rocking back and forth again where she sat. It was silent, even the corridors were quiet. 'You said you never got anywhere with piano,' she stated.
Ezra nodded and looked up at the piano.
'Do you want a lesson?'
He nodded again and the two of them sat back at the piano. He placed his fingers over the keys and Eden moved them to play a C major chord.
'Now press down,' she ordered.
He played the chord, it sounded royal and magical.
'Now, play these notes.' She played a set of four notes individually. Ezra copied her.
'Now put it together.'
He played them slowly and steadily, focusing hard on the notes. His brow was furrowed as he looked down at his fingers and the piano keys. When he finished he chuckled, he was proud of himself.
'Now, try this,' she played the next part of the song. He focused hard, failed once, twice, and on the third go, he got it. She continued to play the next part, and he copied her. She was perfect, he was rusty and slow, and there were wrong notes and missing notes, but you could tell the song.
'You know, maybe you should be a piano teacher. You've got the skills,' he spoke as he finished another section of

the song. Eden thought for a while, it wasn't a half bad idea.

'Maybe I will,' she shrugged. His face was cute when he concentrated hard on something.

Eden had no idea why she was teaching him *Love of My Life*. He wasn't the love of her life, he only played that song to her on the train. They would've probably never spoken of it again if she hadn't brought back up again just now. Was it instinct? Was it really the first song that came into her head when she said she would teach him something? Why not *All of Me,* or *Someone Like You?* A song they had never listened to together and didn't have any meaning to them.

The door opened and someone walked in behind them. Eden turned her head sharply to see who it was.

'I thought I heard talent.' Ms North the music teacher stood in the doorway, smiling with her pearly white teeth. Eden stood up and gave her a hug. At least this was a teacher she liked.

'Sorry, I just thought I'd drop by, say hi to everyone,' Eden said as Ms North let her out of her grip and adjusted her glasses to sit perfectly on the bridge of her nose. Ms North was old, but not too old. She was nearing retirement in Eden's eyes, but would probably never retire until she dropped dead one day. She wore a long brown skirt that looked a bit like a sleeping bag, and had a thick cream jumper tucked in. She wasn't the most flattering lady, and she definitely didn't have the best taste in style, but her warm heart and kind spirit made up for it.

'Don't be sorry my dear, it's lovely to see you. How are you? How's New York?' Ms North questioned her and walked towards the empty chair by the piano stool where Ezra still sat, watching the two of them.
'Oh you know, it's been fun.' Lie. It's been awful.
'And who's this dashing young man?' She pointed at Ezra, who looked up when he felt a brush of air against his face as she pointed.
'I'm Ezra, Eden dragged me up here.' He held out his hand for her to shake.
'Not as bad as you thought it would be I'm hoping,' Ms North joked.
'Not at all.' He smiled, but Eden could tell he was just being sarcastic. It's a shame old people don't pick up on sarcastic humour as easily as the younger generation.
'Well, I've got a class now, but it was lovely seeing you again.' Ms North waddled out of the music room and shut the door behind her.
'She seems nice.'
Eden was just glad she didn't mention anything about her and Archie. She was their biggest fan it seemed. She wasn't even sure if Ms North knew about their whole 'situation'. However much she knew, she didn't want her knowing any more.
'Do you want to grab some lunch?' Eden asked as she stood up from the piano stool. She had had enough of teaching Ezra the piano, and enough of being in the school.
'From the school canteen?' He looked out into the corridor and assumed that people were heading to get food.

'No silly, I know this cafe downtown you'll like.' She took his hand and walked him out of the music room and out of the school. Whatever she had planned to happen in the music room, it hadn't worked. Ezra was still cute and sweet, and had the best sense of style, but he was still just Ezra. She wasn't trying to make him into Archie, you can't change a person. She just wanted to feel like she was falling in love with Archie all over again. And maybe by reliving her past, she could do that.

When they walked into the town there was a food festival happening and they decided to eat there instead. They walked around the red and white marquees that had been set up and breathed in the multitude of scents that the food gave off. There was a cheese stand that had every variety of cheese imaginable, and more, and cake stands with cakes you didn't even think were possible to create stacked up on each other. Pizza ovens and hotdogs stands, burgers and burritos. Eden wanted it all. There was a live band playing in the square, some local people that Eden had never heard of. They were good, but not good enough. Clearly that was the reason they had been booked for an Iowa food festival instead of touring the world.

'What shall we feast upon then?' Ezra said as they made their way through the maze of food stands. The music was too loud for Ezra to hear what Eden said, even if they were standing right next to each other. It was like they had been thrown into a mosh pit at a concert, they could barely move through the crowd of people, and they couldn't hear themselves think clearly.

'We could get a burrito and go and sit somewhere else?' Eden shouted into his ear. He nodded, and found themselves at a stand that sold over priced burritos. She was pretty sure it was a scam, no burrito should cost over ten dollars, and yet here they were spending twenty on two.

'Do you have any idea where we could take these?' He asked in her ear as she handed over the cash and walked away from the market.

'There's this lake just a little out of town. I'd love to take you.'

Eden knew exactly what she was doing. She put her hands in her pocket and felt around for something. It was there. She held the pebble tightly in her hand, before letting go and taking the burrito back from Ezra. He didn't need to know why. They got a bus up to the edge of town, and then walked up the road for a while before turning off down a path. Eden could see the lake now, even in broad daylight it sparkled like it had diamonds at the bottom.

Twenty One

Coming to the lake gave Eden a rush of nostalgia and belonging. It was where the beginning started in her eyes. If the music room didn't work, then the lake would. She wanted the lake to work. The lake sparkled like there were stars and galaxies in it. When one died, another one took its place. A cycle of shining magic. The stars were Eden's map, she knew that they were leading her somewhere, she just didn't know where. They drew pictures in the sky, mystical designs that led her to her fate. Cosmic love worked on two things. Luck and fate. Eden wanted luck to be on her side, but she knew deep down that the only way forward was following fate. What a wicked thing fate was. To run you out of town into a deserted emptiness of nothing. The only luck she ever got was the luck that she survived that day.
They walked closer to the lake, it grew bigger as she neared it. There weren't many people there, dog walkers mainly, and even then, there weren't a lot. She wanted to

find the spot where she and Archie had been, everything had to be exact.

'So, what is this place?'; Ezra asked and looked around at the scenery. The air was so warm they started to regret wearing their coats. It was the first semi-decent warm day where they didn't need to put a dozen layers on just to feel mildly alright. She held out her hand and led Ezra down to the embankment where the tiny waves lapped up onto the sandy shore. There were broken twigs and branches that had fallen from the trees during the storms. Eden always wished that one day she'd find one of those bottles with a message inside asking for someone to save them and then Eden would go and rescue this poor lost soul who had got trapped somewhere. Today wasn't that day, but maybe sometime in the future.

'There's this more secluded beachy area just up the path, we could go there,' Eden suggested, and they walked further up the rocky path and down the hill again to a quieter area. It was so private and silent they could hear the fish move from inside the lake. Eden looked around for the exact spot she had sat with Archie. Just by the tree stump on the small patch of grass. It looked like a gravestone, it just stood there, as still as a flamingo when they stood on one leg. She could feel the warm wind in her loose hair. She hadn't put it up today, because when she came here with Archie, she had worn it down. It was going to get knotted and messy, but that was the thrill of it all.

'Okay,' he let out a big breath as he took the landscape in, 'what exactly is this place?'

'The Black Lake, I discovered it a few years ago, and fell in love,' Eden said.
'But the waters so clear, why is it the Black Lake?'
Eden shrugged her shoulders.
'I think because when the sky gets dark, it looks like the night sky.' Eden bent down and moved her fingers through the water. 'It's an old quarry, so no one really knows the true depth.'
'So a bit like a black hole?' He chuckled and submerged his hand in the water as well.
'Yeah, a bit like a black hole,' she murmured.
They ate their burritos on the bank in silence. She hated hearing other people eat food, but she didn't know what to say. Plus, it was rude to talk with your mouth open.
Eden stared out over the Black Lake/ Black Hole. She liked the new name. It wasn't as clear as it usually was, you could never see the bottom either, people sometimes called it the bottomless lake because it went on for ages. To date no one had managed to dive right down to the bottom, Eden didn't even want to try.
But she wanted to get in. She wanted to submerge her whole body in its icy cold water. She wanted to feel frozen and like she was being sucked into the black hole. She could feel the gravity already pulling her towards it, its pull was strong and it didn't let her go. Eden pulled off her coat, and then her jeans and jumper until she stood there in her underwear. It was pink and beautiful, and Ezra couldn't take his eyes off her.
'What are you doing?' He asked as she ran her fingers through her hair to try and get rid of some of the knots.

'Going in obviously.' Her body was pale and thin, and Ezra thought he could see her heart beating up and down, left and right under her glass skin. You could see the blue veins in her wrists, and her collar bones stuck out just below her neck. She looked like a skeleton.
Ezra slowly started stripping down to his boxers. He peeled off his coat, then his shirt and tshirt, and then pulled his trousers off of his legs. The wind turned and there was an icy blast that brushed across their skin, making them shiver and freeze.
Eden smiled, and then ran across the grass, through the dirty sand and waded into the lake water. It was colder than the air, it ran up her spine and froze her brain. She looked behind her at Ezra, who stood there, his eyes fixed on her limp body.
'Are you coming?' She called after him.
'I don't think I can, it's so cold?' He rubbed his arms across his body and shivered.
'What are you so afraid of? There's no sharks,' she shouted again. Her smile was permanently frozen, she couldn't move it was so cold. Even from a distance Eden saw Ezra roll his eyes and waddle into the water, his arms still wrapped up to his shoulders. She watched the water rise up his body until he was standing in front of her, the water just below their shoulders.
'Not being good enough,' he said. Eden was confused. She tilted her head and looked at him.
'What about that?' She asked.
'You asked me what I was afraid of.'

Eden looked down into the water, she wanted to see her feet. She wanted to see the stars.
'Oh, well...' her mouth didn't know what to say.
'What are you so afraid of?'
'I... I don't know,' she replied. She knew what she was afraid of, but she couldn't say it.
'There's got to be something that makes you scared,' Ezra pointed out.
She shrugged her shoulders and turned around in the water, wading out deeper until her feet couldn't touch the bottom and she was swimming.
'God Eden you never tell me anything.' He followed her through the water until they were both afloat.
'I tell you everything,' she blurted out. The water got in her face as she kept herself above water.
'I don't want to know about your town. I want to know about you. I know nothing. You're a walking talking mystery.'
Eden gulped and let the water cover her head. She stayed there as long as she could, holding her breath until it burnt like a fire in her lungs. There was a fire in her lungs anyway, it was only a matter of time before the fire spread and took over her whole body. Just living started the fire. People watched her burn into ashes, and then be reborn, and do it all over again. It was only a matter of time until there were no more ashes to piece her back together. She brought her head back up and let out the breath she was holding in. Her chest moved in and out as she fought to take in any oxygen around her. Ezra watched, perplexed.

'What's wrong with a little mystery?' She looked at him, his hair was still bone dry and curly.
Then, he dunked his head under the water, she watched him hold his breath and she counted the air bubbled that came from his nose. She could see everything, the water had cleared and she saw him holding his knees tightly to his chest as he stayed underwater. Eden sank below the water too and took his hand. She opened her eyes and tried to find where he was. His eyes were looking into hers, even through the water. In her mind she could hear music being played, like there was a palace under the water that was playing music. It crawled into her ears and got into her mind. She didn't like it. Eden surfaced the water and breathed heavily, Ezra followed her too, and before she knew it he was kissing her. The water dripped from his forehead and into her eyes. His lips were wet from the water as she kissed them, her arms entangled around his neck. She didn't feel anything. Just his lips on hers and his wet hair.
She got out and sat back down on the grass, wrapping her coat around her shoulders to try and dry herself.
'When I woke up this morning I definitely didn't think I'd be swimming in a lake, almost butt naked,' he joked as he followed her up the bank. He covered his shoulders with his coat and brought his knees up to his chest.
'Neither did I to be honest.' She rocked back and forth trying to battle the cold. There were deep dark clouds in the sky that had covered the sun and the lake had gone back to being only somewhat clear. He sat next to her

cross-legged and tried not to show how cold he was, because all he wanted to do was be with her.
'Do you think I'm strange?' She asked quietly. Her fingers picked at the grass in front of her that had been sodden in lake water.
'Strange is a very difficult word to interpret. I'd say you're strange as in mysteriously strange. I know nothing about you, and yet I don't want to know anything. I like how strangely dazzling you are when you just want to be alone. Or how you play the piano strangely beautifully because I've never heard anyone play it as amazing as you do. You're strange because you choose to be on the outside, no one ever chooses to just look at everything instead of being in it. I don't think you're strange as in you look strange. You're mesmerizing, and I think deep down you know that. You're strange because no matter how hard you try, you can't hide how you feel.'
Eden listened to him speak. They were the kindest words anyone had ever said to her, and yet somehow she hated them. Every single last word. She hated them. She despised them. Because those words were only the catalyst for him falling in love with her.
'We can go if you want,' Eden said after a while. They had been sitting there on the wet grass. Barely speaking. Asking questions, not getting much of an answer from either side.
'It's nice just sitting here, if you don't mind,' he added.
They had dried off enough to put their clothes on, but when they did it felt wrong. Like they were putting on another layer of skin. You don't need two layers. So they

stayed put in their underwear. His body was like snow. Soft and cold. She could see bones inside of him and he breathed. There were scars on his stomach, marks where he had had surgery. He was skin and bones, and that was all he was. She looked at them deeper, their markings indenting her as well. And she knew she had made a mistake.

He noticed her staring at him, and he wrapped the coat around his body even more.

'When I was fifteen I got juvenile myelomonocytic leukaemia, or just JMML. They… they did surgeries, I can't really remember, but I'm fine now.' He smiled and opened his coat back up.

Eden knelt forwards and brushed her fingers against his scars gently. She knew then that he wasn't just falling in love with her. He was falling in love to survive. Eden felt ten times worse. Like a cannon had just hit her. If she broke his heart then she would break her own too.

'I'm so sorry,' she shook her head and brought her hand back to her chest. He kissed her again, everything went quiet.

When he pulled away she was crying, again. But the problem was, he thought she was crying at him. He wiped away her tears, just as Archie used to do. Then, she reached down into her pocket and pulled the pebble out. It was round, it looked rounder than usual. Her feet walked her to the bank of the lake and looked out. She wanted it to swallow her up whole, like black holes usually do. She turned the pebble round in her hand and felt the breeze against her bare stomach. Her whole body was frozen, but

she had been frozen in time for so long, what was the difference?
She knew what she had to do. And so she did it. She watched the pebble fall through the air and then make a *plop* as it hit the water. It sunk down deep, it was being sucked into the black hole. It was back home, at last. She turned around and walked back up the embankment to Ezra, who had put on the rest of his clothes. Nothing had changed. She thought that getting rid of the one thing that bound her and Archie together would help her let go. The rocks under her feet dug into her skin. He could've picked up any of them, but he chose that one. And she wished he didn't.
They walked back up the path they had come from and onto the road again. The bus came and collected them, and dropped them off close to her house. Why was it that the first warm day they had had that year suddenly turned into the coldest? She shrugged at herself and opened the door to her house. Inside it was warm, but that was because you could make a house warm. The fire cracked at the fireplace, the table was set for dinner, and suddenly Eden wasn't hungry.

Twenty Two

The next morning dawned on her like a new era. But it didn't feel like a new one. It just felt like another day where she'd have to face reality.
'Whattup dawg?' Juliet said through the phone. She seemed happy, but you can never really tell how someone is feeling through the phone, because the face shows the most expression.
'Nothing much, just chilling at the house,' Eden answered. She lay back on her bed and let her body sink into the sheets. Her towel was wrapped tightly around her after her morning shower.
'What's been going on up there? Any murders?' She joked. Eden rolled her eyes sarcastically.
'You know nothing happens up here. It's Iowa stupid.'
'Very true,' she heard Juliet say.
'What have you been up to anyway?' Eden asked, although she knew it would consist of going to class and making out with Jason.

'Oh you know, writing, reading, ordering takeout most nights,' Juliet listed. That was so unlike her, she loved to cook.
'But you love cooking? Why are you wasting so much money?' Eden sat up in her bed, holding the towel that was still around her, although she was basically dry now.
'Yeah well I don't really have anyone to cook for right now,' Juliet continued saying. Eden put her phone on speaker and started getting dressed.
'What do you mean? I thought you'd be having Jason over like every night.' Eden pulled on a pair of blue washed denim jeans and a green sweater that covered most of her neck.
'Yeah well me and Jason aren't exactly on speaking terms.'
Eden stopped what she was doing and rushed to the phone, throwing herself on the bed and picking it up to her ear again.
'What do you mean you're not on speaking terms?'
'We had a fight the morning after you left, I couldn't tell you what about, but I don't really want to talk about it,' she explained. Eden could hear her sigh on the other side of the phone.
'Okay well do you think you'll be okay? Like was it bad?' Eden asked. She felt somewhat bad that she wasn't there for Juliet, but she knew Juliet was strong, and brave, and the most wonderful human being on the planet.
'I'm sure we'll be fine, we're just having some time apart. I wish you were here though.'

Eden lay back down on her bed and let her head sink into the pillow.

'Soon, I promise.'

'Alright, well I gotta get to class, but I'll talk to you later,' Juliet said. She made kissing noises down the phone and they laughed.

'Bye, I love you.'

'I love you too.' She hung up the phone and rested it on her chest. Even with closed windows she could hear the wind rush by and it brush through the empty branches of the trees. The leaves were never going to grow if the wind continued to live on this earth.

Today her plan was easy and simple. She would go to the snowman field, even if there were no snowmen because it was the end of February, and then she would go to the clearing in the woods. And bring a picnic because that's what she did with Archie.

She descended the stairs and already was facing her worst nightmare. She could hear voices in the dining room, her mother's voice, and Ezra's. They were sitting opposite each other at the table, a full plated breakfast at the place mat and freshly pressed coffee in the middle.

'Eden, hi! Who were you talking to?' Her mother asked and pulled up a chair next to her for Eden to sit.

'Juliet, just checking in on me, or rather me checking in on her.'

'She okay?' Her mum served a plate of bacon and eggs and poured her a cup of coffee.

'Thanks, um yeah she's fine,' Eden lied. Her mother didn't need to know about Juliet's personal life, yet alone her own.

'Good, I haven't seen her in ages. What's she up to nowadays?' Her mother was clearly in the questioning mood this morning.

'Nothing much, just studying, going to class.' Eden started eating.

'Good.'

No, it wasn't good, but it was better than Eden. There was a silence for a minute where the three of them were eating. She could hear the food going around in everyone's mouth and it made her want to be sick. They weren't sloppy eaters, she just couldn't bare the fact that it was so silent you could hear everyone's movement.

'I've been telling Ezra here about you when you were younger,' her mother started speaking after finishing her plate of food.

Shit. This could go one of two ways.

1. Her mother could spill all of the beans about her relationship with Archie and that would make Ezra never want to speak to her again, because like he said, he was afraid of not being good enough. And no offence to him, he was nothing compared to Archie.
2. She could actually be telling him about when she was seven, when she used to dress up in her green coat and yellow boots and pet farm animals and take karate seriously.

She hoped it was the second one. And it was. But not about the farm petting, or the karate, or even why she thought her fashion choices were the next Vogue cover. She told him about how she was an *angel child* and that she was always top of the class for everything. Way to cheer on your own daughter Mrs Harper.
'Fascinating,' Eden rolled her eyes, but they didn't see. Good. One less drama to deal with then.
The breakfast table was always awkward, but Ezra being there increased the awkwardness tenfold. She sipped her coffee, finished her breakfast and then went upstairs. She could hear Ezra following her up the stairs.
'Where are we off to today?' He asked and shut the door to her bedroom behind him.
'All in good time my friend.' She regretted saying it as soon as the words left her tongue and bounced into the atmosphere. He knew what his reaction was going to be like.
'Friend huh? So all those times we made out, they were just, fun?'
She knew he was joking, but part of her told her that it hurt him. She didn't want to hurt him. I guess it was just too late to stop.
'They were definitely fun,' she replied. Her legs were crossed on her bed and she looked up at him. He stood over her like a giant, he wasn't a giant in reality. It was just a simile.
'Were they as fun as this?' He lent closer and kissed her, pushing her down on the bed and pressing his body against hers. She laughed as they kissed. But it wasn't

fun. She didn't think you could have fun whilst kissing someone and not actually loving them. That's why Ezra enjoyed it so much. Because he loved her. Eden waited everyday in anticipation to hear those three little words come from his mouth. She wanted to know for sure if he really loved her.

'Come on, we've got places to be.' She pushed him off and slipped her black boots onto her feet, then grabbing her bag and Ezra they went downstairs and slipped out of the front door before her mother could see.

Eden had to figure out which bus they were taking to get to the snowman field, there were too many to decide which was the correct one, and she didn't let Ezra help, because she wanted to surprise him. It wasn't really a surprise as much either, it was a field that didn't even have snow because it was February and not December, when snowman season was at its peak.

The bus took them up the straight road just west of the town. She wanted to walk the exact route she and Archie walked, over the hill and then straight down to the field where she had built Joe Cocker. It felt weird even thinking about it. When the bus left them at the stop Eden looked around, there was nothing. Just endless rows of fields and nothingness.

'Is this the right place?' Ezra asked as he followed her gaze across the horizon. She saw the hill.

'Definitely.'

They started walking. The grass was rough and shaggy, like uncombed hair, coarse and emerald green colour, waving back at you in the wind, rustling in the breeze. It waved like people in a stadium waved and caught the light that showed how it wasn't just one shade of green but a multitude of colours. Were it summer, Eden would have loved it even more, but the wind blew away any hope of adoration, just like it blew away Archie.

Their legs moved in unison as they walked up the hill, each step was a step closer to looking out over everything all over again.

They talk about everything and nothing. Eden could tell he was falling hard in love, she could see it in his eyes. It was the same look Archie gave when they fell in love. They sparkled like a thousand shining stars. She saw stars in his eyes, but not the kind she wanted to see. Dead stars. Shining dead stars that lit up his eyes. She didn't even think dead stars could shine that brightly. She thought that once they burned out they fell from space like leaves fall from the tree, except they keep falling because space has no beginning and no end. Just an infinity of darkness. Was that where she was heading?

The silence was one she hated, but she didn't want anything else. Just the feeling of being with someone, alone, on a hill, going somewhere she loved. He looked extra adorable today, maybe it was because he wore a hat that flattened his curls apart from the ones that escaped and shaped his forehead. Eden had never noticed before but he had freckles, or moles, that you could play dot-to-dot with. She had never looked at him the way she just had, and she feared she never would again.

They broke the surface and stood at the summit of the hill. The fields below looked like tiny squares you see when you're on a plane and you're lucky enough to get the window seat. Eden always got the window seat, because she liked feeling big and on top of the world when she looked down at everything.

'So, where do we go from here, leader?' He chuckled and held his hands in his pockets.

'That field, just there.' She pointed to the snowman field. It was empty. There was a locked gate at the entrance and heaps of hay bales stacked up one on top of each other.

'That's what we walked all the way here for? A field?' He exclaimed. But he didn't know the meaning behind this field.

She wanted to run down the hill like she did with Archie, so she did. Her legs went faster than she imagined, the wind rushed through her hair and hit her face sharply like blades of glass. Ezra ran down next to her, he was faster and sleeker, like a cheetah. When they reached the bottom they were so out of breath they couldn't speak. She breathed heavily, hoping to get more air inside of her. Her chest beat up and down and she choked on herself.

'How do we get in?' Ezra asked through the heaving.

'Over... the gate,' she replied heavily.

'But, isn't that trespassing?' He pointed at the sign saying *No Trespassing*.

'Technically when I last came here you were allowed in because it's open to the public in December,' Eden explained.

'But it's February.'

'So, let's pretend it's December.' That's exactly what she wanted to do. Pretend it was December and she was creating Joe Cocker the snowman with Archie.

She jumped over the gate and walked into the middle of the field. It was cold and fresh and Eden remembered that she had forgotten to put on the ugly Christmas scarf with sprouts and elves and santas all over it.

'It's not much really is it?' Ezra pointed out as he walked towards her.

'No, it's not. But I like how quiet it is here. You don't usually find places as quiet as this.' She felt the ground beneath her and then sat down, her legs stretched out in front of her.

It is the stillness that will save and transform the world.' Ezra quoted.

'Eckhart Tolle,' Eden looked up and smiled. He sat down next to her.

'You know your quotes.' Of course she knew her quotes. She spent hours on Pinterest looking up depressive sad quotes to try and make her feel better.

'I wonder if I will transform the world,' she said.

'Everyone transforms the world one way or another. Otherwise there is no world. Just an empty ball of dirt and water. We all make a difference, we just don't know it.'

She thought, she hadn't made any difference yet. She was waiting for the right moment.

'What do you want to transform?' She asked him. He looked up into the sky, and then back at her.

'The way we love. The way we love as an adventure, more than a rule. Boy meets girl meets the world meets the universe. '
Eden listened and then realised. He wasn't loving her normally. His mind was whirling through the universe, when hers was stuck firmly on planet earth.
'That would definitely change the world,' she smiled. She let her head fall to the ground and she looked up at the grey clouds that covered the universe.
'What do you want to change?' He lay his head on the ground next to her so they were then both looking up at the universe.
'You've changed the question now, from transform to change,' she pointed out. He laughed.
'Fine then, what do you want to transform Eden Harper?'
'The stars,' she replied quickly. 'I want to replace them with memories. Because I get bored of looking at the same memories over and over again.' She was being hypocritical. All she did was replay her old memories in her head until they were carved into her skull.
'I want to do that too.'
They lay looking up at the sky until they got too cold to stay still for much longer. He gave her his hat he was wearing. It covered her ears, and she was warm. They always say if you keep your head warm, the rest of your body will become warm. On this occasion, the universe was right. They walked back up the hill and as she did so she purposefully dropped the photo that man had taken of her, Archie and Joe Cocker the snowman. It blew away in the wind, but nothing had changed.

Twenty Three

When they got on the bus Eden rested her head against Ezra's shoulder and closed her eyes. He wrapped his hand around hers and squeezed it tightly. It gave her butterflies inside her stomach, because no one ever squeezed her hand like that. She listened to the wheels of the bus turn and breathed in his heavy smell of aftershave. It was like a montage out of a film. The bus driving down the dusty road back into town, two people holding each other like there was nothing else to hold on to. Eden felt like she was in a film. This wasn't normal, her life was like she was following a script. She read the lines and the stage directions, and she did it. She was a puppet in her own film.
When they got back home Eden realised that they hadn't been to the clearing in the woods, but she didn't want to go anymore. Not with Ezra.
They sat on her bedroom floor, the pack of cards shuffled in front of them playing a game.

'How long do you think we'll stay for?' He asked. He put down the ace of spades. Eden shrugged her shoulders and looked at the cards in her hands.
'Couple of days maybe. I want to go somewhere first, and then we can go.' She presented the six of spades.
'Where is this place?' Six of diamonds.
'I think I'd rather go alone. I need to clear my head.' Nine of diamonds. He looked up at her, and then placed the three of diamonds on top.
'Sure, is everything okay?' He watched her look at her cards.
'Everything's fine, there's just something I need to do.' Three of hearts. Eden could tell he knew something was up. He was asking questions.
'Thats… cool,' he replied. Ezra didn't look at her, he kept his gaze fixed on his cards. Her phone buzzed on her bedside table and she reached over to grab it.
Hi Eden, it's Camille. I've found a psychiatrist and booked an appointment for you, next Wednesday @3pm. If you want me to come with you just tell me. And then the message was followed by the address of this place. She didn't want to go. She didn't need someone to tell her she was depressed, she knew she was. Eden threw her phone onto her bed and turned to face Ezra again. He placed the eight of hearts on top. Eden looked at her hand, she had never placed the queen of hearts before. She placed it on the pile.
'Last card.'

He looked up from his cards and then back at them. Two of hearts. Eden dropped her card onto the pile. King of hearts.

'You want to play again?' She gathered up the cards and started shuffling them in her hand.

'In all honesty, I'm kind of tired,' he said and stretched his arms above his head and yawned.

'We could just relax on my bed, watch a film?' She suggested as she packed away the cards into its box.

'I think I'll just go to sleep.' He stood up from where he was sitting and hugged Eden.

'Night,' she whispered into his ear.

'See you in the morning.' Ezra walked out of her room and into the spare room he was sleeping in.

Eden climbed into bed and pulled the covers up to her shoulders. It was only nine at night, but the sky was dark and yet she couldn't fall asleep. Her head was spinning with everything that was happening. She wanted to dream, but her eyes didn't let her sleep. Why was it that something so simple became so hard when you actually wanted to do it? Eden began to beg for something that was never going to stay. It never intended to stay. Why did Archie do things like this? Flip you around, turn you inside out back to front, make you fall in love, and then expect you to be okay when everything is imploding around you. It's not normal, people don't act like that normally.

Before she could even comprehend what was happening Eden was out of the house, running. She ran up the road and out of town, and up the road even further. The icy cold air but her skin like shards of glass, but she ran through it even still. The sky was so dark, the clouds had covered the stars and the moon. It was pitch black. Her eyes darted back and forth as she ran, she could barely see where she was going.

Eden turned off down a dark track and started to walk. She brushed her fingers along the bushes, they felt like thorns sticking into her skin. The path widened and she was in the clearing, just as she had been when Archie brought her here. She could hardly see anything, the darkness covered everything, the trees, the grass, the flowers, everything. Her bag felt heavy on her back. She threw it onto the ground and then bent down to unpack everything she had put in it. A ten metre ball of string lights, powered by batteries, every single photo frame she had pushed under her bed (and more), her purple dress she had dug out from the bottom of her closet, and the record. Eden unravelled the string lights and scattered them around in a circle until they met again. It looked like she was standing in the middle of a seance, but Eden saw it as her being surrounded by stars and planets. She stood the photo frames up, one frame to every three light bulbs. Eden changed into the purple dress and threw the clothes she was originally wearing out of the circle, along with her backpack. And so it just left her, every inch of her body frozen with cold, holding Archie's record, standing in the middle of the circle. Surrounded by memories that weren't really memories, because all they were, were LED lights she had turned on with two batteries. Eden sat in the middle, crossed her legs, and placed the record on her lap. The string lights illuminated the whole clearing, and soon they were illuminating the tears on her face. Her palms rested flat on top of the record and she started breathing short sharp breaths as she turned her head and looked at the photos she had surrounded herself with. Her lips were blue from the cold and her teeth chattered up and down.

- Her and Archie at the Black Lake the evening he proposed to her, they had set the self timer off on the camera and propped it up against the bottom of the tree stump, before smiling at each other and taking the photo. She was holding the pebble in her hand, you could see it in the photo. She would never see that pebble again.
- A picture of Archie and Joe Cocker the snowman, because even if she had got rid of the photo of the two of them, she had kept this one. His whole face was filled with happiness as he wrapped his arms carefully around the snowman. His cheeks were rosy red from the cold and you could see the ugly Christmas jumper Eden had bought him, under his thick coat.
- Them at Archie's first gig at the local hall where he was the intermission entertainment at some sports event the town was hosting. He had his guitar hanging from his back and his arm around her shoulder. There was a drum kit in the background and a microphone in front of him which slightly ruined the picture, but it only reminded her of how much she loved his singing.

- Both of them on stage performing *The Spring Concert Song* at their school's spring concert when they were in junior year. They were sitting on wooden stools, Archie was playing his guitar, and Eden sat next to him singing the lyrics they had sung together in the very clearing she was sitting in now.
- Several photos of the two of them in Malibu, on the beach, at the restaurant, walking down the streets, Archie with his guitar, one of her in the pink top.
- Them just being all around goofy and silly, photos captured by Juliet who was their personal photographer most of the time.

Eden wanted to keep all of these photos. The tears streamed down from her face, because she knew she couldn't. She had to move on. She couldn't continue loving Archie. You'd think there's only a certain amount of tears someone can cry before they run out of ingredients to make them, but her tears poured down her face. She could taste the salt as they seeped in through her mouth and down her throat. Eden looked round again at what was surrounding her. They weren't memories anymore. They were stars. The lights were the stars, and she was the sun. Her skin grew tiny mountains where goosebumps formed, she shivered and held onto her arms, falling fully to the ground and lying her head on the grass.

Rain started to pour from the sky. It wet her hair and ran through her makeup, making her eyes look black and drowned. The rain soaked into the ground making it slushy and muddy, and it oozed onto her skin, through her bare toes and legs, in between her fingers and on her dress. Her purple dress. Eden heard her phone ring from her bag outside the lighted circle, but she didn't leave. She lay there, letting the rain cry on her and letting her cries rain on the ground. It was her fault. It was her fault she was even in this mess. It was her fault Archie left and it was her fault he hated her. She didn't want to remember the day, but she did. It seemed as though it was the only day she could remember now. She could hear the shouting, the crying, the calamitous minds they had. She could see their apartment, the four walls which they called home together, the paintings they had bought from a flea market, the lamp they had found on the side of the road, the bed they slept on every night, together, as a couple. She could feel the cold wall on her back as she fell to the floor crying after he left the building, the rug that had shedded tiny bits of fluff that blew across the room whenever the door opened and the cold draft swept its way across the floor. Eden saw him standing in front of her as they argued, as they threw comments at each other and stared each other out. He was even more beautiful when he was angry, but she didn't want him to be beautiful, because that made her love him more.

Her hair hung loosely, she looked up at Archie, he was leaning against the window looking out over the view. Endless rows of ugly buildings, all shades of brown and grey. This wasn't what she wanted. She wanted him, and all he wanted was fame. She twisted the ring around on her finger, pulling it up and down contemplating whether she should be even wearing it.

He stood up from the window and walked over to the sofa, slipping on his shoes and wrapping his coat around him.

'Where are you going?' Eden asked, looking up from the table as she read the newspaper.

'Recording studio, I've got to add some extra things in for the album,' he replied blankly.

'Can I come?'

He shook his head, 'I think it's best you stay here.'

On most occasions Eden would let this go and move on.

'Why?' She called after him.

'Because I don't want you getting hurt.'

What bullshit was this? No one was getting hurt.

'Why would I get hurt?' She asked. He sighed as he almost opened the door.

'There's lots of people who follow me, they grab and pull wherever I go. I just don't want you to get hurt,' he explained.

'You know that's not the real reason why you don't want me coming,' she said as she stood up and walked around the table.

'Uh, yeah it is,' he answered. His hair was messy and unbrushed, and he was pale in the face, it didn't look like him. This wasn't him. Nothing about them made any sense anymore.

'No it's not, and i'll tell you why. You're ashamed of me. You don't want people to know who I am, because I'm not famous like you. I'm too plain and normal. I'm too simple for a rock god like you. I'm embarrassing to you, I'm not good enough to be in your image that's portrayed all over the world. I'm not made to be in the spotlight with you.' Her voice was raised and you could hear the anger. He stood there, Eden could see his chest breath up and down and the vein in his forehead emerge as he processed the words she had just said.

'Well that's kind, you're so incredibly kind Eden. You know I've been waiting for you to say that, ever since we came here. I've been waiting for you to realise how little you are in this world, and yet I chose you. I chose you to be a part of my big world, you!' He pointed at her fiercely, tears falling from his eyes. She had never seen him cry, but she didn't care.

'I wasn't kind, I was just telling the truth. You're obsessed. You're addicted to being famous, it's all in your head. The fame, the money, everything. Did you ever think for one minute how I came into this equation called your life? You dragged me to New York like I didn't have a choice. You didn't ask me if I even wanted to go to university, you just assumed that I would be your groupie that followed you everywhere you went. I'm not a toy you can drag around, I'm a human. Did you ever think for one second that maybe I wanted to be like you? Did you ever ask me what I wanted to do? I sit here everyday, watching you on the news, looking through paparazzi pictures, and I want to be by your side. I want to do this together.' Eden stopped speaking and gulped. She looked up at Archie, he looked at her.

'It's not as easy as it looks,' he started saying.

'What's not easy? The singing? The music? Archie I don't want to be your big secret from everyone. You never would've even got this far if I didn't push you.'
'So you're saying I don't deserve any of this? You're jealous, because I made it and you didn't,' he shouted.
'I'm not jealous. You're obsessed. If you had to choose between your career or me, what would you choose? The door is right there, because I already know the answer.' She raised her hand and pointed to the door.
'You can't make me choose between that,' he pleaded.
'I can, and I will. I recommend you choose the door, because if you really loved me, there wouldn't even be a choice,' she said through the tears that fell down her cheeks.
'Eden I love you,' he cupped his hands around her face and she pushed them away as she wiped away her tears.
'No you don't. Not anymore. You love the idea of me, what you really love is your career. And I don't think I can stop you loving that. Archie you're my whole world, I love you, but I'm not your world, am I? Every morning when you wake up, you don't think about me, you think about your career. That's your soulmate. And maybe one day, some day in the future, we'll meet like we never met before, and fall in love all over again. We had a great time, and we will have a great time, but for now, it's over. It's just over.' She fell to the floor and pressed her back against the cold brick wall behind her.
'I will never forgive you for this,' he said, and she heard the door slam shut. She didn't even say goodbye. She didn't even watch him walk out of the door. Eden cried into

her hands and rocked back and forth. Her eyes were stained with black mascara and her lips were red and puffy. She looked up to the ceiling, there was nothing. Just like it had always been. She saw the December snow begin to fall from outside the window. Eden stood up, grabbed her bag and packed everything she owned into it. There wasn't much, she had been living in Archie's world for so long she forgot what it felt like to live in your own for once.

Eden curled up in a ball on the wet grass. She looked at the lights, and the pictures, and the darkness in the background. She looked at nothing, because she felt like nothing. Eden lay there in the rain until she didn't even know she was lying there. Because the pain was too hard, and the air was too cold. She wanted to follow her heart, and do the right thing. But her heart was so broken she didn't know which piece to follow. She shut her eyes as if for the very last time and let the rain cover her in all its tears until you couldn't make out what were the tears and what were the raindrops. Her body was frozen all over, and somehow it unfroze for the first time. Now she was in the real world. Eden watched the string lights flicker off as the rain seeped its way into the battery pack. She couldn't see her memories anymore. She hoped that feeling the pain inside of her- somehow- meant she was doing everything right and her plan was working. But she didn't have a plan. Just ten metres of broken string lights and a dozen old photo frames that held pictures of someone who was never going to forgive her. She couldn't move, so she stayed there, in the wet, cold, night, her teeth chattering against each other and her eyelashes forming icicles.

Twenty Four

She was being carried in someone's arms when she woke. The feeling of being lifted above the ground by someone scared her. Her hair was clumped together in knots and her skin was dry from mud that had solidified itself. She couldn't feel her toes, but she knew that the wind was blowing lightly through them, and her legs had several cuts and bruises on from falling to the ground. She looked up. Ezra's face was determined, to get her where though? She didn't want him to know that she was awake, so she went back to sleep. Her eyes shut and all she could see were stars and planets. She was placed into a car, the heating cranked up until even she was overheating, and the car moved. It was early morning, seven maybe? The fresh February morning blew cold breezes and let birds sing in the trees. She could hear them, but she didn't want to.
Eden didn't say anything the entire car journey, she didn't know where she was, or where she was going. She wasn't even sure how Ezra had found her. Had she been out there all night? She took short sharp breaths in that sent

the redness back into her lips. For a second she thought she was dreaming, this hadn't really happened to her, this wasn't her life, she was just dreaming. She watched Ezra drive her mother's car down the road she had run up the previous night, her eyes flickered open and closed, she didn't want to see. Eden couldn't face the thought of seeing Ezra again anymore. He probably knew everything about her. All the tiny details about her life. Why had he even come to get her if he knew? So she closed her eyes again, there were stars painted on her eyelids, big bright ones that blinded her. Was this what it felt like to be crazy?

He placed her down on her bed and brought the sheets up to her chin, sponging her face down with warm water and gathering her hair together so that he could loosely tie it up. She wanted to cry and show him that she was there, but she had run out of tears to cry. Eden watched him walk out of her room and close the door behind him. She heard his footsteps walk down the staircase, and then she heard the front door close. He was gone. Maybe for real. Everything had gone wrong. Everything had come to bite her, because she had floated so high above the water now, that she couldn't get back without any help.

She fell asleep again, her eyes glueing themselves shut because she never wanted to open them again. She couldn't face the damage she had caused any longer. She was about to break Ezra's heart, and she knew it. She sat up in bed, the morning was now the afternoon, the rain fell lightly on her windows. Eden reached out to grab the pack of cards that sat on her bedside table. She tipped them out into her hand and shuffled them gently so as not to bend any. They were smooth and delicate and felt like calm waves between her fingers. She began to analyse each picture card, the jacks, the kings, the jokers, and the queens. Eden always thought she was the queen because doesn't everybody want to be a queen, but in reality she was just a joker. A joke to the world.

Her door opened, Mrs Harper walked in with Eden's bag, and everything she had brought to the circle last night. She had left it there, her phone, everything.

'Bought you a present.' She dumped the bag on the floor, and then fished out her phone and placed it in front of Eden and the pile of cards she had in front of her.

'Thanks mum,' she smiled weakly. Mrs Harper sat on the edge of the bed and sighed deeply, her chest rising up and she breathed out and then in again. Eden noticed the dark bags under her eyes and the tear stains that marked her pretty face.

'Eden what were you thinking?' She finally said, reaching her hand out to Eden's and rubbing it between her fingers. Her mum stroked her fingers on Eden's skin, all the way from her forehead, across her cheek and down to her chin, smiling, relieved that Eden was just alive.

'I don't know mum. I don't know,' she shrugged and brushed her hand against the cards that were now scattered across her lap.

'We were so worried… and your father… he was scared to death something had happened.' Mrs Harper started crying, the tears rolling down her cheeks and onto her lap.

'I... I'm not sure what happened. One minute I was here in bed and the next I was running and I couldn't stop,' she muttered quietly.
'You're so precious. I just can't face losing you,' her mother brought her hand up to Eden's cheek again and held it there. Eden wanted it to stay there forever. And then she realised, how did Ezra even find her?
'How did you find me?' Eden asked, confused.
'Ezra managed to track down your phone. Said you'd had a conversation earlier about how you wanted to go somewhere, alone. Figured that it would have something to do with that,' her mum explained. They looked at each other, holding on to their hands, and crying.
'I'm so sorry, I don't know what was going through my head,' Eden spoke after a while. Her mum let go of her hands and rubbed her legs up and down. Eden thought she would start to make static electricity if she didn't stop.
'Eden you've got to let this go.'
'That's the thing, I can't. I've tried, so hard. I brought Ezra here to see if I could love him, I got rid of everything, and I still can't forget him. It's like he's found himself a little corner in my brain and he's not leaving. I can't move on, I can't,' she blurted out. Eden brought her knees up to her chest and let the cards fall off of the bed and onto the floor.
'Maybe you should stop trying to forget about him, and just let it happen. Let him slip out of your mind naturally,' her mum replied.
'I don't think I can do that. I can't stop loving him. He was my first everything, it's not that easy to just forget.' Eden

rested her head on the back of the bed, letting out a big sigh as she did so.

'Tell me everything,' her mum kicked off the shoes she was wearing and climbed next to Eden, wrapping her arm around her shoulder and bringing her in for a hug.

'Mum, I really don't think I can talk about it,' Eden rolled her eyes and nested her head on her mother's shoulder. She felt like she was four again and she had just come home from her first day at school and didn't like it because she didn't like not being with her mother the whole day.

'I'm your mother, you can tell me anything, you know that right?' Mrs Harper ran her fingers through Eden's knotted hair and breathed in the smell of her washed face.

'Do you think soulmates exist?' Eden asked, digging her head further into her mum's warm aroma until she thought it was hurting her. Being close to her mum felt like hugging a huge bear, because her mum was soft and strangely beautiful.

'I think love exists. Soulmates is just a silly phrase that people use to explain how much love they feel. There's only so much love you can give before it starts breaking down, so you have to balance it. You met Archie when you were only sixteen, the odds of you finding a soulmate at that age are almost nothing, but you loved each other so much, you didn't care if you were or weren't. Because being in the moment was all you cared about.' Her mother smelled of old roses pressed into a bottle and then sprayed all over her. She liked it.

'He used me. He used all of the songs he wrote about me to become famous,' Eden stated.

'He didn't use you, he took the pieces of your relationship and showed everyone something beautiful and new,' Mrs Harper explained.

'Maybe I just got lucky.'

'It's all love is. Luck.' Her mum closed her eyes and pulled Eden in tighter. Eden remembered the time when she used to compare cosmic love to either luck or fate. She used to think fate was her version of love, but maybe it was just luck, maybe it had always been luck?

'I keep thinking that the stars are our memories, and they hold our love. But maybe there's nothing up in the sky but air,' Eden murmured. Her voice was heavy as she spoke, like she was being forced to say it. But it all clicked in place. If there were no stars, then cosmic love wasn't real, and she was just fantasizing over something that was never going to happen.

Eden shut her eyes and thought. She tried to remember a time when she was truly happy, it was with Archie. They always were. She was happy because she got lucky. Eden always thought that their love was fate, because that's what he told her. But all she got was a handful of luck for two and half years and an eternity of tears.

She lay there with her mum, thinking about everything and nothing, because it was all she had to think about. She wasn't going to get over it, she realised that now. Because with luck comes anger and sadness and all of the bad emotions mixed into one. She hated him, but she wanted him more than anything.

Her mum left her and walked out of the door. Eden stood up and collected the cards together on the floor. She

emptied out the bag which was full of the pictures she had brought with her. The lights were wrapped messily around them, like someone didn't even care if they broke them or the frames, they just wanted to pack it all up and get rid of it. Eden stood each photo up on her floor and looked at them. She was lucky that someone had captured each moment so beautifully. And then she knew who went back and cleaned it all up. Ezra. He had gone back and collected everything that was left. The lights, the pictures, her phone, her clothes. Everything. She jumped up and thrust open the door, but Ezra was already there, about to knock. His fist was clenched tight together and Eden could see his rings on his knuckles. She stood still in the doorway, looking at Ezra. He dropped his fist and stood there in front of her, as if they had met for the very first time. She turned around and walked back into her room, the frames still propped up, scattered across the floor. Ezra looked down at them, and picked one up.
'Ezra I…' Eden started saying.
'Save it. Your mum told me everything,' he uttered. His head was bent over the photo he was staring at. Eden didn't even want to know what photo it was, because she knew everything had changed.
'You know when I met you, I thought you were sweet and charming. You had this mystery to you, that I didn't care about, because I had never met someone like you before. But this mystery that you were, you love him. I don't know what I was to you anymore,' he confessed.
'Do you hate me?' She asked through the tears.

'That's the thing Eden. I can't hate you, I love you. But what does that say about me?'
'I don't... I don't know,' she muttered.
'Exactly, you don't know. You never knew anything about how I felt. I saw us moving in together one day, going on vacation, having date nights at restaurants, and all you were thinking about was him.' He wasn't shouting so much, but upset, angry.
'I'm sorry...' she cried. She broke down onto the floor surrounded by the photos of Archie and her.
'Why did you even bring me here?' He dropped the photo onto the floor, the glass smashed and Eden saw the picture. The Black Lake. No more lying.
'I thought... maybe I could fall out of love with him, and in love with you. All the places I took you, he took me to, and that's how I fell in love with him,' she confessed.
'So you thought that you could relive the past with me?' He crossed his legs and sat on the floor, picking at the shattered glass and placing it on the dressing table next to him.
'I thought I could fall in love with you... but I can't. I just can't.' She shook her head and wiped her wrist against her eyes, trying to dry them. There was silence, she watched him pick up the remaining shards of glass. She wished they could cut her right now so that she could feel the pain. Anything would feel nicer than what she was feeling in that moment. After a moment he spoke.
'Do you miss him?' His voice scarcely a whisper.
In three words she broke his heart.
'All the time.'

Eden watched Ezra leave the room. He shut the door behind him, but to Eden it felt like he was shutting the door on life. Like she was separated from the universe. She fell onto her bed and cried into her pillow. It seemed there was a separate tank of tears for Ezra. Her pillow was wet with salty water when she sat up. She was still wearing the purple dress, now covered in patches of mud, and ripped up the leg just slightly. Eden picked up the frame on the floor of her in the dress. She felt sick just looking at it, like there was a different girl smiling back at her. Eden threw it on the ground and it shattered into pieces, the glass cut her leg and feet. She didn't care. She picked up another frame and threw it violently to the floor. Her body started sweating as she broke each frame, it dripped from her forehead and onto the floor, mixing with the ink from the pictures.

She heard a car pull up outside the house and talking going on from behind the window. Eden ran over the broken frames, the glass splitting her skin as it cut through the layers. There was blood coming from her feet and legs, she ran down the stairs, leaving bloody footprints as she did so. The door was already open, she ran out onto the stone steps and watched someone open the car door. Ezra stood there, his back to Eden, and holding his backpack in his left hand.

'Ezra!' she shouted. He turned his head, looking at her, and then turning back to face the car. 'Ezra wait!' She ran across the stone path that led up to her house and stopped before him. Her feet were cold against the stone and they were now covered in fresh red blood.

'You don't have to leave, stay please,' she begged. Her hair had fallen out of the bun Ezra had tied it in and it hung freely around her neck.

'Eden, I think it's best,' he replied, throwing his bag into the back of the car and climbing in.

'Ezra please, can we talk?' She pleaded.

'About what?' He pulled his seatbelt across his body and clicked it in place.

'Us.'

'There is no *us* anymore. I don't think there ever was,' he replied.

'It doesn't have to end like this.'

'Eden, be honest with me, did we ever really start?'

That hurt Eden like a knife going through her heart in a million different places.

'Do you love me? If you really loved me, you would stay,' she said as she let her tears loose again. And then Eden realised this was exactly how Archie left. She had spoken the exact same words, all over again. Would she ever move on? Was this the way every relationship would end?

'Eden I love you so much that I have to go. Because I don't think I'll ever be able to look at you and not love you.'

'Then stay,' she pleaded, 'stay.' She held onto the car door so that he couldn't shut it.

'Why? Why do you want me to stay? You're only going to make me fall in love with you even more and make it even more impossible for you to love me,' he argued. Ezra undid his seatbelt and stepped out of the car again. He towered over Eden like Goliath did over David, but in reality they were both Goliath, because she was a monster that was out of control.

'Because I can't be alone,' she cried. Her shoulders bounced up and down as she cried more.

'Tell me you love me. Tell me, and then I'll stay,' he demanded softly.

'I can't,' she shook her head and her hair shook with it, 'I can't do that.'

'Then there's no place for me here. Not in this town, not in your life, not ever.'

'Ezra please,' she bawled, 'just let me explain.' Brick by brick her walls came tumbling down. They crashed to the floor and broke all around her. Why had it taken so long?

'Eden I need to go,' he started to get back into the car, but she grabbed his arm and stopped him.

'You once asked me what my favourite colour was,' she gulped as she looked into his eyes, for the very last time. 'Archie's favourite shade of pink.'

She let his arm slip away as he got into the car. He shut the door and the car rolled away like in the movies where they play sad music and the car leaves, leaving Eden standing at the side of the road, broken. She watched the car all the way down the street, until it turned off to the left, and Eden was standing there alone. Her feet were covered in dry blood, and there were cuts in the soles that killed as she walked back up the path to her house.

She fell asleep listening to *Love of My Life* because that was her and Ezra's song. She was never going to see Ezra again, but something in her heart told her she was okay with that.

Twenty Five

'Mum, dad,' Eden walked into the living room and sat down at the sofa next to her dad. He had been watching some form of sport on the TV and her mum was knitting. Typical. They looked over to her, her arms were neatly placed on her knees and her posture was immaculate.
'I need to go back to New York,' she spoke. Her parents looked at each other, her dad took off his glasses and her mother placed the knitting down on the coffee table in front. Their eyes met with uncertainty, like Eden had just said something illegal.
'Honey I don't think that's a good idea,' her mother said.
'You're not ready, not yet,' her dad added.
It had been three days since Ezra had left. The early days of March had come and Eden could already see the leaves starting to blossom on the trees. She didn't want to miss it in New York.
'I actually need to help Juliet,' she stated. The room was dimly lit with yellow lamps in the corner and the fireplace was slowly warming up the entire room.

'Eden do you really think it's what's best? What with… well, everything.'

She sat there and thought, just like she always did. Was it the best thing to do? Ever since she moved to New York her life was turned upside down and flipped inside out. Everything bad that had happened, happened there. But it's where she wanted to be.

'I've got a flight booked tomorrow morning, you can't make me change my mind.' She stood up and left the living room, walking strongly up the stairs and into her room. Her bag was half packed with everything she was taking. It lay on her bed, the contents slightly spilling out of it. She picked up the album, the cover was ruined from the night it had spent out in the rain, she hoped it hadn't ruined the vinyl itself. Some of the blue sky dripped and the stars merged into the blue, making it one big mess. The outline of Archie faded, she couldn't tell where the drawing began. It was a catastrophic image of wonder. She ran her fingers across the picture, sketching out the man with her fingernails. She wasn't going to cry, not this time. Eden flipped the record over and read the contents one last time. She traced each song out, humming it gently in her head.

- *The Brightest*
- *Mercury*
- *You are so Beautiful*
- *Follow my voice*
- *I can't lose you*
- *The Spring Concert Song*
- *Loving Someone Like You*

- *Malibu Hotel*
- *Love Song*

And then one more. One she hadn't heard of, one she didn't even realise was on the album. It was the title of the album. Eden had never listened to it, because she never made it that far into the tracks before she turned it off. She could never make herself listen to the entire album, because listening to it was accepting the fact she and Archie were no more. Eden searched for her record player, and then remembered. Shit, it was in New York. She carefully opened her door and went into her parents room. They had one above the chest of drawers, old and vintage. It's box was brown and sleek and was heavy to carry. She held it in both arms as she carried it back to her room, pushing the door open with her foot and then resting it on her bed. She slid the vinyl out of its sleeve and onto the deck, pressing the needle down and tuning it in. It crackled like a bonfire, and then played. Eden didn't want to listen to any of the songs apart from that one. The one she hadn't heard.

She lay back on her bed, as she always did and closed her eyes. The music was different, it didn't fit his style, it wasn't like the other songs. It made her want to shred every single bone in her body, and rip out her heart, squeeze her lungs and stamp on her brain. And yet she wanted to lock it in a box and keep hold of it forever. She tried to listen to it like she used to listen to Archie play whenever he performed a new song. But she couldn't, because he wasn't there. The music sank into her like a ship sinks at sea. Like the Titanic sank, tragically beautiful. Snapped in two and sank right down to the bottom. She played the song over again, analysing each lyric like it was poetry in an exam. She defined every word, what everything meant. Every song had a meaning to it, people just never bothered to work out the true meaning. But more than anything, she liked listening to his sweet mellow voice that played through the speaker. His rough, hauntingly beautiful voice that played the song. If she listened closely enough she could hear his fingers picking at the guitar strings as he sang, confined in that recording booth months ago.

Eden had always watched the films of people who slowly go crazy. She watched them so closely that she became one. She felt there were radio waves buzzing around her head, dark voices and the lone truth that she was going mad. All of her ideas came from the voices, the good, and the bad ones. All she had to do was choose the right from the wrong, the good from the evil. She had to choose love over hate. But hatred over what? Herself, or Archie? Eden brought her hands up over her ears and tried to block out the sound, it was hurting her with its irresistible waves of noise and music. She rocked back and forth on her bed, her forehead sweating and her skin too hot to touch. But she was still hot. Eden pulled her top over her head and unthread her legs from the jeans she was wearing until she was there in her underwear. But she was still too hot. She looked around her room for a fan of some kind, something to cool her down. Nothing.

Eden ran out of her bedroom and into the bathroom, tightly locking the door behind her and turning on the yellow light. The tap poured ice cold water as she twisted them on, like she was about to go swimming in the Arctic Sea. Eden dipped her toes in to check how cold it was, but to her it was warm. Lukewarm water, like the stuff that's left out on a hot summer's day for too long and then you're forced to drink it kind of warmth.

Then, after minutes of contemplating whether she should actually get in, Eden submerged her entire body into the water, it covered her bare shoulders, her pale, stick thin bone structure, and her cut feet. She let her hair fall into the water, it went two shades darker and straightened out immediately. Her chin hovered above the surface just as the dragonfly hovered above a pond. She felt like she was in a pond. Cold but not really cold water surrounding her. Eden's eyes closed shut, she took a deep breath, and then submerged her whole head under the water. She could feel the water run up her nose and into her ears, but she didn't open her mouth. That would be suicide. Eden let the fire burn up again, even longer this time. She let it rise slowly from the ashes, taking in all the oxygen that she had in her body. Eden watched it form, it was the greatest cinematic experience she had ever seen, because for once, it was real. And then it started to burn, and she could feel the burn, but she didn't want it to stop. She wanted to keep on burning until everything had burned out. Eden held her breath longer, and opened her eyes. The water was murky, and she could barely see through it, just the rough outline of her body, her pale skin, and the plug at her left hand. She draped her fingers over it, she wouldn't pull it. She would keep burning. She

laughed at herself under the water, she was burning in water. Usually the water was the part that stopped the burning, not intensify it.
She couldn't hold it anymore. She realised she didn't want to die, because she didn't want to be killed by water. There were other, much greater and scarier things to earn your death. She pulled the plug and let the water drain off of her. She didn't move, she let the water do that part. Her wet, naked body lay in some weird shape in the bath. As she climbed out she took a look at herself in the mirror, and then punched it, causing the glass to shatter in front of her. Her knuckles cried with blood as she brought her fist back, there were cuts just like on her feet. Why hadn't Eden realised by now that glass was her enemy, and that her fragile body couldn't handle the amount that was slitting her body in two.
She wrapped a towel around her, and then one around her bloodied fist. It looked like someone had just smothered tomato ketchup all over it. Eden walked to her room and closed the door quietly behind her so as not to wake her parents. She didn't know what it felt like to go crazy, until now. Her mind was telling her everything at once, and she couldn't keep up.
What was she going to do? Where would she go tomorrow? Should she kill herself? Do you think Archie is thinking about me? Is Ezra thinking about me? What's the best way to end your life? Which way to the Black Hole? Am I strange? Do you think I'm normal? Do soulmates exist? Is there anything in the sky but air? Am I a stranger?

She texted Juliet quickly.
Coming back tomorrow around 2pm, will you be in?
Eden threw her phone onto her bed and dressed into her pyjamas, the oversized ones that Archie had left at her house once, she found them in the wardrobe two days ago. They smelled like him, and when she put them on a little part of him was with her. She felt like he was sleeping with her when she wrapped herself in the pyjamas. She was close to him again, finally. Her phone buzzed as she pulled her hair into a bun, and wiped the remaining mascara off her eyes.
Yes! I'll tidy the place up lol, can't wait to see you.
Eden typed her reply imminently.
I reckon it'll get messy as soon as I walk in again. Don't even bother! I've missed you!
Putting on a fake show was the least of her worries, of course she missed Juliet, they were best friends, but something inside told her that she should continue missing Juliet. Trying to act happy when everything was imploding was her worst fear.
My lonely self has missed you even more she thinks. I've watched too many Harry Potter's, over the limit of eight films in one sitting if we're confessing.
Eden laughed at that, silently, but she laughed.
I don't ever think you can watch too many Harry Potter's. They're cinematic masterpieces, all eight of them.
She eagerly waited for a reply, watching the little bubble thing move up and down as it showed Juliet was typing.

Trust me, I think Harry Potter and the Half Blood Prince three times today was slightly too much. I'm slightly obsessed with Slughorn now, oops!
Eden's fingers moved quickly as she typed her reply.
Please never be ashamed of watching Harry Potter too many times. It's a pure talent to be able to do that.
She smiled and watched her phone receive a reply.
I'm glad someone finally appreciates my talent.
Eden left her on read, because she forgot to reply. She got distracted by something. By Juliet. She felt so bad for her, how she fights everyday just to keep Eden alive, and as a friend. Eden treasured their friendship, because despite everything, Juliet didn't want to lose her. She looked at the photo of the two of them on her wall she had stuck up years ago. She looked at the faint pencil lines on her door where they had marked how tall they were over the years. They had faded, but Juliet had always been taller, and Eden was incredibly jealous. Eden pulled down the photo and removed the blue tack from the back. She folded it in half and pressed it into her bag, ready for tomorrow morning. Her heart raced, because everything she was doing tomorrow, was everything she should have done months ago. She looked out of her window into the dark, rainy night. The street was dead with silence, and the cars looked like tiny bugs parked on the road. She closed her curtains, but something caught her eye. Years ago, even before she met Archie, she had gone through a weird phase of writing quotes down and leaving them in strange places. She had just found one, written in tiny handwriting on her wall at the bottom of the window sill. It

had been hidden behind potted plants and photo frames, but now she saw it. Her eyes were widened. It was that stupid quote from the film Angelina Jolie was in:
Happy endings are just stories
That haven't finished yet.
Clearly back then she could predict the future. Why the fuck were happy endings even dreamt of if they were never even real? Why can't people just admit that happy endings don't exist, because one day, we're all going to die, and all that's left will be dead stars and planets and a whole load of nothing.

Twenty Six

Eden cradled the record in her arms when she arrived back in New York. She sat on her fold out bed in the living room, cross legged, and held it close to her chest. She didn't want to listen to any of the music, because listening might just kill her.
'What happened with you and Ezra?' Juliet asked as she held two hot mugs of tea in her hand, one for herself, and one for Eden. She sat on the end of her bed and smiled at Eden.
'I don't think I can talk about it,' she sighed. Her arms were cold and had formed goosebumps everywhere.
'From what I can gather, I have a pretty good idea of what happened. Just know you can tell me anything.'
'I don't know what went wrong. What did I do to deserve all of this?' Eden took a sip from the hot mug. It burned her tongue to a crisp, but the pain was over quickly, and soon she didn't even realise it had burnt.
'It's just life. It'll be over before we know it,' Juliet shrugged.
'I suppose.'

They wrapped blankets around them and leant against the wall, cradling each other like a mother cradles her baby.
'You okay?' Juliet whispered.
Eden wanted to say yes, because lying was her second, and now first language, but she didn't. Lying was now out of the equation. Running on the truth was now the only thing keeping her alive.
'No, but I'll survive.' Maybe that was a lie, she didn't know. That was the problem, in the end, Eden didn't know anything.
She climbed the stairs, they were metal and made funny clanging noises as her boots hit the surface. The lights flickered on and off as she pressed her feet onto each stair. She looked down at how many she had climbed, she was at least six floors up, and there were three left. Eden kept climbing the stairs, pressing her hands into the pockets of her jacket. There were old wrappers and receipts which had made tiny piles in the corners. She tipped them out and let them run down the stairs and stop at the landing. It was cold, but wasn't it always? Eden could hear the music, and she could hear him. His singing was something she would never, ever forget.
She pressed the cold heavy door open. The room was empty, apart from a small spotlight, a guitar, and a boy. Archie. He hadn't noticed her, so she just stood there, listening to him play the music. He looked different, his hair was wet and it rang out his sweet curls which usually fell in front of his face. There was black under his eyes, and a silver chain around his neck. The entire room was empty, like he was standing in a void of space and time.

There was something so grungy and punk about him that Eden didn't think it was him for a second. She didn't think someone could drastically change in a matter of months. She watched his mouth move as he sang, his fingers strum the electric guitar that hung around his shoulders. There were short sharp breaths coming from her mouth as she fixed her eyes on him. The light around him caught the guitar and made it shine into a thousand pieces across the empty room. She stepped further into the darkness, closer to the light that circled him. Her eyes started to cry, but she wasn't sure what of. Nothing was happening, and that was the point. Nothing happened when she saw him. Everything carried on as it usually did. She didn't feel anything, only resentment towards herself. The tears fell down her face again and onto her top. The pink one, Archie's favourite pink top. It made splashes in the material so it looked spotted, or as if it had a tie dye effect. She walked further into the room, her body surrounded by the darkness. He saw her. Maybe the pink gave it away. The music kept playing, and he kept singing, but this time she understood the lyrics without having to hear them. Because she knew what the song was about.

Archie stepped off the stage and walked towards her, the cables draped behind him as he held his guitar. He stopped two metres in front of her, his face was hot and sweaty, just like hers. The fire in her heart burned viciously and brightly, so brightly that it ignited his fire and they found eachother in the dark. Because even in the dark, she could hear his heartbeat.

In this universe, and in this galaxy, in this world, we as humans are reincarnated to fill this empty void with our loneliness and our fight to be together again. We found our way to each other and to be loved by one another, but our love was so cosmic and interdimensional, it failed us. It failed to exist in this world's bullshit, so we left the world too. And one day, we hope to meet again, in another dimension, a world where our love will be worthy enough to survive. And when we do, every single world will watch in awe and astoundment.

They stood in front of each other, he had stopped singing, but the music played on. It echoed throughout the room, throughout the building and into the night sky. She thought that maybe the whole city could hear the music, that's how loud she felt it in her ears. She saw him gulp, his neck moved as he swallowed the saliva, and he blinked heavily, brushing the hair out of his face. She hated him, but she wanted him.

'Forgive me,' she whispered, but she was sure nothing came out of her mouth. He turned around and walked back up onto the stage. His black top clung to his back and she could see the sweat marks that stained it. He placed his guitar back in its stand and clenched his hands around the microphone in front of him. His lips were almost touching it, they were stained a bluey black colour, how Eden wished she could be touching those lips right now.

Archie started to sing, she had never seen him sing without the guitar, it was realer, and rawer than ever before. His voice was husky as he sang, there was grit in it and felt like there was something stuck down his throat. It was another song. A different song. A goodbye song.

Forgive me for I didn't know
That we were so young
And lost in love
Now I understand how much I took from you
We were anything more than we could've planned

When everything breaks down
You pick up the pieces from the ground
We played a game with luck and fate
But maybe there's nothing in the sky but air
No preternatural design
No cosmic love destined for our lives

Everything you find has already been found
Because with everything we've been through
It seems the strangers always you
And we're alone again
In some alternate universe
That we called our own

Because fate was never in our hands
We learned to live
And then we died
And you were always the stranger I thought you were
Goodbye cosmic lover
Goodbye, my friend.

Eden broke down into a well of tears, falling to the floor in the empty room that she had been standing in. It was cold and dark, so darkness she became. Eden saw stars that held her memories. Each star showed her something she had experienced, how her life was important and that life had meaning. She could connect each one, dot to dot, like a game, until the very last one. It was left hanging, like nothing could connect to it. Different. Eden tried to reach out and grab it, but she couldn't. It was all in her head. She could feel the fire burning inside of her, she could feel his fire burning, but they didn't meet. Not anymore.
Eden reached inside of her coat pocket and felt for the ring. It was there. She clenched her hand around it and brought it out of her pocket. The knuckles on her hand had gone bone white, you could almost see the bone itself. She gulped, and then walked slowly up to the bare stage, watching her feet as they moved one in front of the other. Her fist unclenched and she placed the ring in front of his feet. It reflected off the spotlight, and blinded her eyes. She never thought that giving up something so small and meaningless would make her cry that hard, but it made her realise something. It was over.
Eden turned around and headed for the door, she didn't even look up to Archie, who had been watching her the entire time. His adorable blue eyes, and his curled hair that Eden used to wrap around her fingers. She was never going to see him in the flesh. And you know what. She was okay with that. All this time she had been scared of seeing him, because she knew that when she did it would be the last time, but everything made sense. Every single

piece of her heart was pulled back together in a broken kind of way for one last day. Because in the end, she didn't want to die of a broken heart, but of a broken life. 'Eden wait,' she heard him say. She turned around one last time. He was walking, no, running towards her, his black shoes pressing silently into the floor. Eden watched his hair bounce up and down, and the chain around his neck swing from side to side. This wasn't Archie Kingston anymore. This was Archer King, the young rock rebel who Eden used to love.

He stood in front of her, she could feel his warm breath on her face, his forehead drip with sweat, his chest beat up and down like a drum. She wanted him to kiss him, one last time, so she knew what it felt like to love someone. 'What? What is it?' She muttered behind the tears. He breathed even more heavily, like he was gasping for oxygen in the atmosphere.

Eden felt like the four walls surrounding them had just been blown away, they tumbled down like the Berlin Wall and she felt the wind rush through her hair. She looked up at the stars and the planets. How beautiful they were, in all their shining wonderfulness. And then she realised that he was right. There was no cosmic lover preassigned. Nothing was written in the stars, just their names on the list of people that had been born into the world. Because there is nothing in the sky but air.

She looked at him, his eyes were blank, just as they always had been, she just didn't realise it before. She never wanted to realise it. Eden had been so reluctant to tell the truth because she couldn't accept the truth that was so blatantly obvious to her.

His body was limp and weak, she could push him and he would fall over easily. He looked away, closed his eyes and gulped. She saw a tear fall from his face, she thought he was strong, but clearly he was, and always will be, a little boy with a broken heart.

'Goodbye,' he whispered, or mouthed. Eden couldn't tell over the music that was playing in the background. He turned and walked away, into the darkness, nothing was the same. She watched him walk away, desperate for him to turn around and think he made a mistake, but he didn't. She knew she couldn't follow him this time, she had to follow her heart.

Eden pounded her feet against the metal staircase again, still going up. She was out of breath and needed air. Her mind was racing with a multitude of different thoughts, and yet she couldn't think straight. She hadn't been thinking straight in months. Eden tried to trace back to where it all began, what started it, what really tipped her over the edge? The breakup? The overdose? The record? Or was it Ezra? Sweet, innocent Ezra. He was probably in his teenage boy bedroom playing video games or listening to *Songbird* or *Love of My Life* because he was that kind of boy who would obsess over a song for weeks. She missed him, because he gave her belonging, but he also gave her pain. She couldn't look at him and not see Archie. And what was Juliet doing right now? Trying to reconcile her relationship with Jason? Cooking dinner for the two of them? Watching another Harry Potter film?

Eden climbed the stairs still. What was Camille doing right this moment? Entertaining her four children? Trying to get Eden to go to a psychiatrist? Eden didn't need a psychiatrist. What she needed was Archie, and yet she couldn't have him. Camille had done everything to try and help her, and yet nothing had worked. She wasn't bipolar, she was broken, Eden had known that since the start. And what would Mr Shore do now that she wasn't going back to work, ever? He was so bubbly and bright, and he loved Eden as much as he loved his store. Eden saw him as like a second father to her, he made the world a brighter place, she thought.

The metal stairs finally ended and she thrust open the door to the roof. It was cold as she walked out, there were satellite spires in one corner, a loose chair and nothing else. It was empty. The New York skyline was lit with wonderful lights and noises. A city of dichotomies, exhausting and exhilarating, humbling and inspiring. It's hard itself to even set a love story in New York, when the only love story ever written is when you fall in love with the city. She breathed in the heavy fumes of the city and listened to all the tiny voices on the streets below. It was dark, no one could see her. The sky was clear that night, the moon was full in all its glory. You could see the dark craters if you looked closely enough.

She stumbled further onto the roof, everything around her felt like it was staring at her closely, watching her every move, when in reality, nothing could see her, and nothing ever did see her. She was invisible.

Nothing could save her now, she listened to the thoughts in her mind, telling her different things, but one stuck out. Nobody wanted her. Everybody wants to lead an extraordinary life, people are capable of doing magnificent things, but no one takes the chance. She slipped off her jacket and folded it neatly on the floor. Eden placed her phone carefully on top, and then sat cross legged in front of it. She wanted to write something, but what with? She didn't bring any paper, or a pen, or anything to tell them how she was feeling. All the empty receipts she had kept in her pocket were scattered down the stairs she had just climbed up. Eden rocked where she was sitting, her jeans soaking up the wet puddles that had formed on the roof. She looked like a tragic mess. Her phone powered all the way off in the cold wind, Eden looked up at the stars, again. How wonderful they shined, she wished she could be one. She wondered what it would be like to be a star. People look up to you every day, they tell you how pretty you are, how beautiful, you precious. You're taught about stars in school, she wondered what it would feel like to have your name taught about in school. People drew stars, she always wanted to be drawn, in paint, ink, pencil, chalk. They always looked so pretty, she thought. Eden wanted to grab hold of a star and keep it forever. She blinked, and then stopped looking up. She stared out over the skyline, the wind brushing through her hair like her mum brushed it when she was younger. She missed her mum, and her dad, and her home.
Eden stood up, her arms were numb from the wind and her lips had turned a shade of dark blue. She walked

slowly to the edge, peeking her head over the top and staring down. There were a few people walking past, a street lamp which flickered on and off, and two yellow taxis waiting to collect someone. Her knees were shaking as she stepped onto the ledge, her eyes were blank, but full of expression. She loved what she saw. It was beautiful. She kicked her shoes off and placed them next to her coat and phone. She could feel the cold stone ledge on her toes, it gave her shivers. Was today the day? Would she finally let the fire burn out completely? The date was March 5th, was today a good day to die? She stopped questioning herself, because any day was a good day to die. Some people don't even get the choice to die or not, it just happens. Eden looked closely down at the streets below, and then up at the stars. They were the last thing she wanted to see when she died.
And then she fell.

Twenty Seven
(three months later)

The water broke as she dived in from the rock. It produced little white ripples across the surface and then bubbled away as soon as they arrived. The water was so pure and so clear that she could see everything. She thought she could see the bottom, but that would be impossible, surely. There were tiny lake fishes swimming around her feet as she trod the water keeping herself afloat. Juliet dunked her head under the water and pushed off from the rock, gliding and cutting the water, pretending that she was parting the Red Sea. Her skin was smooth and pretty against the water as she swam further into the centre, holding her breath until she couldn't any more. It was a warm summer day, there were families dotted all around the lake, across the embankment, little children playing on the sandy areas, groups of teenagers jumping from the rocks into the water. Juliet had never seen the water so clear before, it felt like she was swimming through a pool of glass.

She watched the sun set in the west and lay flat across the body of water. People started to disperse as they went home for the evening, but she stayed. She closed her eyes and floated further out into the lake, not caring how far she went, because she knew that one day she'd be back. From where she lay she had a perfect view of the sun slowly melting away. Dripping drops of fiery orange and tangerine gold below the horizon for someone else to enjoy. And although the sun was dripping fast, the daylight lingered around in the air, as if it was accidentally left behind. It was a work of art. How God created something so beautiful every night she did not know, she didn't think anyone could create something so perfect and majestic, and never fail. It was a work of art, colours spread across a canvas, as if those rays were destined to create a work of art each time. She was in awe, because everytime she watched it, she watched it as if for the very first time.
Her palms rested flat on the surface of the water and her hair spread around her like seaweed in the ocean. She smiled, breathing in the freshness of the summer evening and breathing out serenity. She hummed softly with the birds, and the fish, and the sound of the water lapping up onto the shore. It was a gift to even be allowed to float endlessly on the surface that should be kept perfect forever.
She pulled herself out of the water and onto the rock she had jumped off of. The water dripped off and made little pools in the tiny craters of the rock. Her blue towel lay spread out on the rock, she climbed onto it and rested her head on her bag, looking up into the sky and trying to

count the stars. She had always admired the stars, because everyday they appeared, and sometimes you couldn't see them, and sometimes you could, but they didn't complain. They were always there, always shining and twinkling in the sky, despite only being seen for a short amount of time, because when they do come out, everyones asleep anyway. Maybe that's why they came out at night, because they want all the beauty for themselves. Selfish little fuckers. But that meant they saw the beauty in us, just like we see the beauty in them.
The air stayed warm all evening, like there was a permanent central heating fan that just blew warm air all over her and showered her in glorious heat. She felt her damp skin, and ran her fingers through her dark curly hair. This was why she came home. For this.
The good thing with turning up five hours early is that you get to experience everything, and not just the evening. She got to feel the real sun instead of the lingering warm air the sun had left behind when it set. She heard footsteps behind her, she was expecting them. Juliet wrapped the shirt she had worn around her shoulders and looked out over the lake. The space next to her was taken by someone sitting down, he too looked out and sighed.
'It's even more beautiful than I remember,' he spoke.
'It's always been this beautiful,' she replied. Juliet turned her head to look at him. The wind caught his curls perfectly, and the remaining sun bounced off his face making it glow.
'How long have you been here?' He asked calmly.
'Five hours. I was in the water.'

Archie blinked and stretched his legs out across the rock.
'Did you swim down to the bottom?'
'No one can swim to the bottom, it's infinite,' she answered.
'Maybe.' He let the air caress his face like a baby, his ears could hear everything, everywhere.
'She's here,' Juliet said, speaking to the lake and its water.
'I know, I can feel her.' He looked at Juliet finally and smiled.
'It's funny, I was trying to remember some of the stupid things she used to tell me, she once said that she wanted her memories to replace the stars. So that she was surrounded by happiness. Don't you think that's just wonderful?' Juliet explained.
Archie picked at the pieces of string and old bracelets he had around his wrist. Some were red, some were purple, some were blue. But one was pink. And it reminded him of her.
'Her head was always in the clouds.' He reached inside the pocket of his shorts and pulled out an envelope filled with pictures of them. The ink stained his hands as he tipped them into his palms, and then he scattered them out on the rock. Juliet looked closely at them, each one told a different story, but they all had her in, and they were all happy.
'She was always so happy when she was with you, I had never seen her so happy before,' Juliet noted. She picked up one of the photos and smiled.

'She liked to see the world.' He smiled and looked at Juliet. She was analysing each photo, because that's what she was best at.

'I think… she taught me how to not judge people on the outside, because she could see beauty in everyone, just not in herself,' Juliet added. Her wet hair dripped on one of the photos, she flinched, and then stopped worrying, because photos fade after a while.

'She taught me how to believe in the impossible, because she was impossible, and yet I still believed,' he spoke.

'I didn't think anyone could be the physical representation of impossible.'

'She was. She most certainly was impossible, and that's why I loved her,' he replied.

'And do you still love her?'

'No,' he said, 'I can't love someone who loved the sky more than me. That's like loving the animal food instead of the animal.'

'But nothing is in the sky,' she said.

'Everything is in the sky.'

They picked up the photos and walked down to the embankment slowly. Juliet let the sand engulf her toes, she let it scatter across her feet and stroke her ankles. The water lapped onto the sand slightly. Juliet and Archie bent down and dropped the photos in the water, letting the waves bring them back and forth until they had reached the middle of the lake. One day they would sink down through the lake, into the unknown, maybe they would reach the bottom, or maybe they'd keep sinking into different universes and different worlds.

Then, Archie reached into his pocket again and pulled out the ring. He held it tightly in his hand and looked out over the horizon, maybe if he threw it far enough it would fall off the edge of the earth. The water covered his toes, he looked at the ring, and then wrapped his fingers around it again. The moon looked fuller than ever, and the stars shined brighter.

'I think she finally got round to replacing the stars with memories,' he pointed out, because they weren't stars anymore. Archie could hear the laughter around her that they had had together. When you feel more in love with the memories than the person, that's when it's over. Juliet watched him throw the ring into the water. It broke the surface, and then fell. The water was so clear that they could see it fall, but he turned away. He didn't want it to reach the bottom.

They walked around the lake five times until it was early morning. By then the sun was completely gone, the moon was in the sky, and the cool air had finally settled on the world. Mostly in silence, because silence was all they could speak.

'You know, she kept your album under her bed. And listened to it every night, but like one song at a time over and over again,' Juliet giggled as she spoke, 'she was your biggest fan.'

'Is… she is my biggest fan,' Archie added.

The dusty path came full circle once more and they were standing by the rock again. He walked over to the tree stump that stuck out of the ground, there was a collection of daisies to its left, and an abandoned shoe someone had left earlier.

'You know, this is where I proposed to her,' he said, and knelt down to sit on it. Juliet stood next to him and they looked over the lake once more.

'She never told me you were engaged, until like January this year.'

'That's because we decided to keep it a secret. Could you imagine what her parents would say if they found out their sixteen year old daughter was engaged?' He laughed and looked over his shoulder at Juliet.

'That's exactly what she said to me.' They smiled like nothing had even happened. And soon, one day, they would smile like that again.

'God I miss her so much,' Archie said, shaking his head and looking down at his feet.

'I know, I know you do. I keep thinking this whole thing was a prank and one day I'll turn around and she'll be there, smiling and waving, like she had just gone on holiday for a really long time.' Juliet sat next to Archie and stretched her legs out in front of her. It was one in the morning, everything was silent, just like she wanted it to be.

'I think she is on holiday, a never ending one, up with the stars, it's all she ever wanted to be. A star.'

'She was a star, she just didn't know it.' Juliet picked at the daisies next to her, running her nails through the slits and the threading another one through it to make a chain. Her eyes started to droop as her body began to shut down. She wanted to sleep, but she would stay awake, for her.

'I promised her a happy ending. I promised her a fucking happy ending, and look what she got.' He was almost angry at himself. He wanted to kick himself so hard that he felt the pain throughout his body.

'That's probably the most stupid thing you can ever promise someone,' she remarked, looking up and rolling her eyes.

'Someone should've stopped me.'

He picked up a daisy and handed it to Juliet, and together they made a daisy chain with all the daisies there.

'You had a happy middle, and a happy start, does that make up for it? She laughed and nudged his knee.

'I sincerely hope so.'

They walked around the lake three more times, because they were alive, and it's all they could do to take their minds off of everything else. She left the daisy chain on the tree stump when they did their final lap. She thought the lake looked pretty at night, because despite the water being so clear, you couldn't see anything. Juliet reached into her bag and pulled out the album, it was still stained with rain water from that night and the case was slightly bent. She handed it to Archie, his hands clasped around the sides of it. He traced the outline like she used to always do, but he couldn't keep it.

'It's yours,' he handed it back to Juliet.

'Wh-... Why?' She asked, confused.

'I gotta let go, I can't hold on to her anymore.' He shrugged, and Juliet took the album back, placing it back in her bag, zipping it up, and then swinging it onto her back.

The lake was dark and black, and had tiny twinkling stars reflected on it. Juliet looked up at the sky, and there was everything but air shining back at her.

SUICIDE PREVENTION

Get Connected- a free, confidential 24/7 helpline for young people under the age of 25 who need help and don't know where to turn. Call: 0808 808 4994 / www.getconnected.org.uk

Papyrus HOPELINE UK- confidential, suicide prevention advice open 9am-12am (midnight) every day of the year. Call: 0800 068 4141 / Text: 07860039967 / https://www.papyrus-uk.org/hopelineuk/

Samaritans- confidential 24-hour helpline. Call: 116 123 / Welsh Language: 0808 164 0123 / https://www.samaritans.org

SupportLine- Confidential emotional support to children, young adults and adults. Call: 01708 765200 / Email: info@supportline.org.uk / https://www.supportline.org.uk/

DIAGNOSING MENTAL HEALTH IN TEENS

Mind- Mental health helpline open 9am-6pm Monday-Friday. Call: 0300 123 3393 / Text: 86463 / Email: info@mind.org.uk / https://www.mind.org.uk

YoungMinds- Helpline for parents. Call: 0808 802 5544 / www.youngminds.org.uk

SURVIVORS

Survivors of Bereavement by Suicide- confidential for those over the age of 18 who have been bereaved by suicide. Open 9am-9pm Monday-Sunday. Call: 0300 111 5065 / Email: email.support@uksobs.org / https://uksobs.org/

Mayo Clinic- An American non profit medical practice and medical research group.
https://www.mayoclinic.org/healthy-lifestyle/end-of-life/in-depth/suicide/art-20044900

AUTHOR'S NOTE

Writing this book encouraged me to learn more, and to help, those struggling with mental health and suicidal thoughts. I was shocked, and deeply saddened, to discover that nearly 800,000 people a year take their own life. That's every forty seconds someone takes their own life. And every forty seconds someone is left behind to cope with the loss. Even though people are becoming more accepting and aware of the nature of mental health conditions, there is still a huge widespread stigma.
In *Nothing in the Sky But Air*, Eden is severely depressed by the idea that she doesn't know how to live a life without Archie, so she just stops trying. Her belief in soulmates overrides the thought of living happily as she comes to the conclusion that she doesn't want to live if Archie isn't there to live it with her. I believe that Eden didn't want to die, but she had no desire in wanting to live, and that is what drew her to taking her own life.
Often, mental illnesses go undiagnosed because people are too afraid, or ashamed to speak up and admit that

something is wrong. In this case, Eden is in complete denial, and doesn't bother to talk about her issues to other people, even though she is given the chance. This is very much the case in our world today. Nationally, around two thirds of people with mental health conditions will go undiagnosed.

A lot of the themes throughout the book come from songs I listened to during the Covid-19 pandemic, which coincidentally is when I wrote it. Specifically, *Wicked Little Town -Reprise*, which comes from, one of my favourite musicals, *Hedwig and the Angry Inch*. The song is a response to *Hedwig's* own version of the song, which shows how he strongly believes in the concepts of cosmic love and how love is preassigned in the stars. *Tommy Gnosis*, the 'soulmate' in this case and also my inspiration behind Archie, tries to explain in this version how *Hedwig* is wrong about the concept of cosmic love and states that he admires *Hedwig* for everything he gave in their relationship, but it's now over and she should move on. He insists that *Hedwig* is only looking into the sky as a scapegoat as fate and luck have no part in deciding who loves who. The song also inspired me to name the book *Nothing in the Sky But Air,* which is one of the lines in the song. Many other quotes are inspired by this song, as it is a song about losing your way after an important relationship with someone.

I don't believe in happy endings. But I think every story has one, somehow. Or at least, there's closure. Nineteen year olds don't get happy endings, they've barely loved. Who am I to talk, I'm sixteen and sometimes think I'm on top of the world, but then also believe the whole world is against me. Just like that stupid quote Angelina Jolie said in a film once: 'Happy endings are just stories that haven't finished yet'. This story is finished.

Of course I could go on and on, but I think the most important, and urgent message, is that no one should be left alone to deal with the thoughts and feelings that Eden felt. I am very proud of this book, and I hope it helps you understand that you are not alone. If you think something is wrong, speak up. Nothing is your fault. Help is here, waiting for you.

Eleanor.

ACKNOWLEDGEMENTS

Thank you to all those who pushed me to publish this. Without your help this wouldn't have been possible. To my parents who had no clue I was writing this until I placed 70,000 words on their desk one Friday morning in June and said 'I just finished this'. My siblings who didn't care what I was doing, because they're just like that. And to my friends who believed in me. To Erin, Grace, Anna, Stella, Niamh, Izzy, Maddie and Leoni. For your endless support I am eternally grateful.

Thank you.

Printed in Great Britain
by Amazon